BLOOD DIAMOND

EL MUNDO DE SANGRE

DIAMANTE DE SANGRE
BOOK ONE

LANA SKY

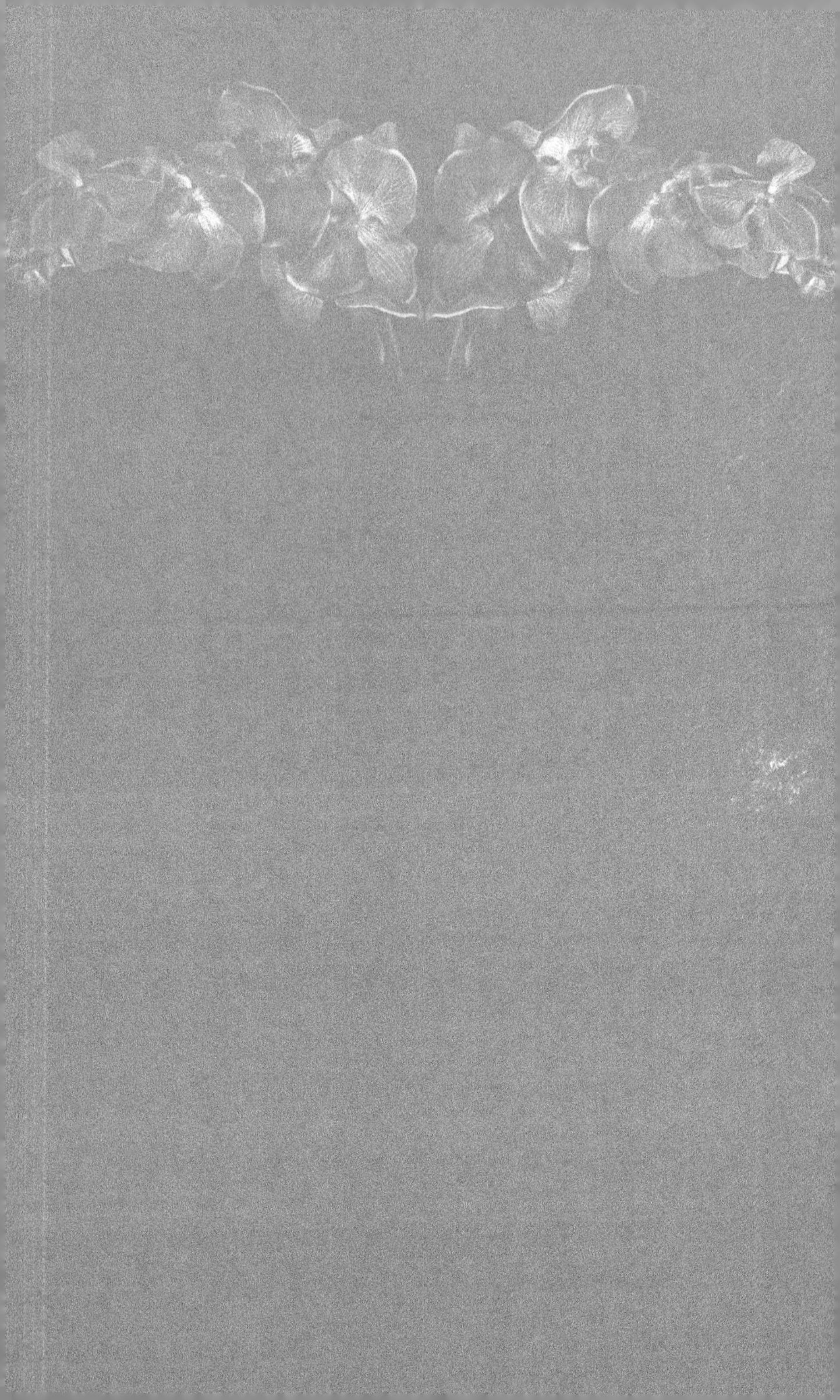

Blood Diamond

Blood Diamond By Lana Sky

Cover Design and Interior Formatting by Charity Chimni
Editing and Proofreading by Charity Chimni

ACKNOWLEDGMENTS

Thanks so much to everyone who supported this draft along the way, including the many beta readers who provided encouragement! Please keep in mind that this story includes dark, graphic, and explicit content matter that may not be suitable for readers under the age of 18—or for readers who are uncomfortable with the following subject matter: explicit sex, mentions of domestic violence, mentions of child abuse, graphic depictions of violence, and mild gore.

CHAPTER ONE

I n terms of morality, I am far from a saint. That's why I'm not afraid to venture alone into Hell—at least figuratively—even if it means risking my life. The fact is that I forfeited my soul a long time ago, but I was damned well before that.

It might be said that I grew up in hellfire. There were more bullet holes in the walls of my childhood home than toys. Being raised by addicts left me with no concept of true goodness, let alone love. What it feels like. Tastes like.

Until the Devil himself "rescued" me, my life was devoid of any genuine compassion. How tragic is that? In that moment—between misery and pain—one man took advantage of my broken soul and fed me a taste of what he claimed was happiness.

Dios mío, I can't deny that it felt like bliss. And agony— there was no pain like it. I hated it. I craved it. My young mind could not comprehend this bittersweet emotion. It can inspire the loveliest sentiments, and drive you to commit sins you never would have imagined.

In all fairness, I've cured myself of that aching, illness of love once. I swore to never let myself be guided by it again.

Several years later, however, I am stripping naked before a man who reeks of stale beer and corn chips in a rundown club. All in the name of love. It's one of the most degrading experiences of my life, and that's saying something.

But I wouldn't have it any other way.

Franco. I chant his name like a mantra, and concern for him alone makes this worth it—feeling inconsistent air conditioning cool the sweat on my bare skin as the man in front of me pats his beer gut with one hand while twirling my panties around the index finger of the other.

Franco. Franco. Franco. With his innocent hazel eyes and delicate features that resemble mine. My sweet little boy. For him, I will endure anything.

"Small tits," the man before me says disapprovingly. "But your ass is fine enough. I'll put in a good word to Hugo's crew, but I don't think they're looking for any more girls. Here—"

I receive my panties and eagerly slip into them before pulling on my shorts.

"Too many risks nowadays," the man adds, "and, no offense, you don't look like a pro, baby."

I fight to conceal my disgust as he smiles to reveal a blackened front tooth.

Damn it. Who knew men rumored to be slavers could be so picky when recruiting fresh bodies? "I really need the money," I say in a tone that I hope conveys desperation.

Too much desperation. The man chuckles and grips the front of his stained jeans. "If you need money, sweetheart, I can help you…if you help me."

"Ah." I don't let my hopeful grin falter. "I'll keep that in mind."

As I walk out of the bar into the sweltering heat, I don't feel as dignified as I would like to think. The truth is, if he had offered me the chance to meet Hugo Garcia in person, I would have sucked anything he wanted. After a raid at the border sent all nearby governments into a state of alert, the narcos have been cautious. Despite Hugo Garcia's arrogance, he can't take the risk of accidentally hiring an undercover cop or reporter who is eager to unearth another aspect of the syndicates' web.

Though, if I were a reporter, I'd be less scrupulous about getting what I want.

A juicy headline isn't in my sights, merely an audience with Hugo or someone with a fraction of his power. While Garcia isn't at the top of the food chain in terms of cartel bosses, he's powerful enough. With his collection of strip clubs spread across the county, he controls the flow of illicit goods in and out of the city. Someone like that would have no trouble smuggling a woman and a child out of the country. In theory, at least.

The reality is he's the last on a dwindling list of contacts I've tried to meet with. It's time to stop playing games in the hopes of catching notice. I'll have to come up with another way to gain the attention of a narco boss if flaunting myself before them isn't enough.

And fast.

The clock on the dashboard of my battered van is a cruel reminder of how little time I have left—just twelve hours before Braulio's gone for good. If I can't find some way of stopping him… Franco will be out of my reach, at the mercy of a man too cruel to ever have custody of a child.

The name Braulio Rivera is enough to frighten even the normal citizens of this city who pretend ignorance of our thriving drug trade. He is as inescapable as a shadow, and thanks to my foolish sister, he's inextricably linked to me by his sole son.

My nephew. When Tiena disappeared a month ago, Braulio cut contact with anyone outside his inner circle and began selling off bits of his operation. Through rumors, I've learned that my hunch is correct—he is leaving tonight with his son. I've been in the game long enough to recognize a cut-and-run when I see it.

Whatever Braulio plans to run from has him spooked enough to reject any attempts to meet. Phone calls. Visits. My last venture to one of his compounds nearly got me shot

—a clear enough warning that I'm no longer welcome in his orbit.

But while he knew my sister intimately, Braulio doesn't know the first damn thing about me—I won't lie down and accept his tyranny without a fight.

I have fought and fought for the last few weeks without gaining any actionable intel. Finding another narco powerful enough to disrupt Braulio's plans and get Franco out of his grip was supposed to be a stupid but *doable* plan.

Hugo Garcia was my second-to-last resort. Only one man remains, but I know better than to attempt to draw his notice... Or maybe I *did* a few hours ago before winding up at yet another dead end.

Desperation leaves no room for logic or fear.

Warily, I drive back to the apartment that's become my unofficial headquarters in this shitty part of Terra Rodea, Texas, and I fashion a new plan. Enough crawling around the outskirts of the narcos' empire.

It's time to dive in headfirst and go straight to the man who rules them all.

The kingpin. The nightmare. The coldest, cruelest bastard in these parts.

I'll beg for his help on my hands and knees if I have to. Or, should he so choose...

On my back.

CHAPTER TWO

S ome men simply can't be characterized by a chilling reputation alone. They have a body count. On the national index of several countries, they have an entire page dedicated to their crimes. The kind of men the law can't touch.

Julian Domingas comfortably sits at the top of that list of infamous narcos. A known trafficker with enough money and influence to rival several small countries, he is a force to be reckoned with, if not the most powerful man on earth. If anyone can get Francisco out of Braulio's hands, it's him. I'd stake my life on it.

Though, I might lose a lot more than that in the end. Fighting a formidable monster sometimes requires allying with a more vicious one. Occasionally, you'll need the devil himself.

Despite the insane risk, I tell myself what a good idea it is. How smart. How logical. How entirely *not* stupid.

As always, Pedro is there to loudly put me in my place. He arrived not long after I returned from the bar, summoned by a frantic text message. After hearing my plan out loud, he laughed before raiding my minuscule liquor cabinet for a bottle of whiskey.

"Jaguar's men would gut you before you could get within two feet of him, let alone ask him to take on a rival just for you," he declares before downing his drink. "You think Braulio's heartless? Just wait. Even trying to talk to Jaguar is suicide. No, it's beyond that, Pita. It's plain, fucking masochism. You have a death wish? Try heroin and booze like the rest of us."

I roll my eyes without comment. Been there. Done that. I rely on a new vice these days, and it seems to be blindly hoping to change my fate with sheer willpower and bad luck. In a sense, it's only slightly less debilitating than any addiction.

"Rumor has it he's a sadist," I reply, thoughtfully biting my lower lip. "A tactic like debasing myself might appeal more to someone like him."

"Oh no." Pedro throws his hands into the air and raises a heavily filled-in eyebrow. Paired with his made-up eyes and short brown hair, even I can admit that he's stunning. "First, you wanted to seduce some low-level sex trafficker in your grand scheme. Now you jump to debasing yourself before a crime lord? Is there nothing you won't stop at?"

"No," I say seriously. We're in my tiny living room, and perched on a battered end table is one of the few pictures I own—one of Franco taken at his school. He's so damn beautiful. So innocent. I can't just leave him in Braulio's grasp.

When Pedro sighs, I know he's followed my gaze to the same image.

"I won't stop," I say softly. "Not until I get Franco away from that sick bastard. There is no way in hell I'll ever let that monster Braulio keep him. Never."

Pedro raises another perfectly-plucked eyebrow. "And Jaguar is any better? Braulio may be a snake, but some might consider a snake a better provider than a...well, a hungry jaguar. Let's say you convince him to take down Braulio and his gang, and then what? He'll let you skip off into the sunset with his rival's pride and joy? It's bullshit, Pita, though I'm sure you already know that."

I raise an eyebrow as well and watch as Pedro sashays over to my kitchenette to grab a handful of ice from the freezer. "You seem to think that I plan on sitting back and letting Jaguar be my knight in shining armor, should I be able to convince him to help," I say. "No. I'll let the snake and the jaguar kill each other while I sneak off unnoticed with a child neither bastard truly gives a damn about. That, my dear, is what you call a win-win."

Or insanity, but I'm already sold on the concept, and frankly, it's the only solid plan I have.

"Besides, I need to strike before Braulio takes Franco from the country."

"I should have never told you that," Pedro says, shaking his head. "Damn me for being such a gossip."

A gossip who gets his rumors from sources he refuses to tell me about. Given his "profession," Pedro has always been able to score incredible intel—no matter how devastating it turns out to be.

"But you did tell me," I say. "After exhausting every reasonable avenue, I need some way to keep him here. I have to try. *You're* the expert on men, Pedro," I add, abruptly changing the subject. Dressed in a low-cut red dress with one nipple brazenly exposed, no one could deny that Pedro has an appeal few women possess, let alone me. Luck or charm isn't the source of his success. No, seduction is a skill he's honed through a life of pain and misery, scrapping for whatever living he could find by any means.

Even though he isn't proud of his circumstances, he is damn proud of having survived to see himself established in a much-better position than where he started. He rarely tells me about his escapades, but his lifestyle doesn't come cheap, and I know the rumors. He deals with powerful men. Even some in the cartels. Perhaps Julian Domingas himself?

The sad part is that I know Pedro won't tell even if he does. In addition to his wits and sheer determination, his knack for discretion has kept him alive.

Even so, he knows a thing or two about seduction, and I'm eager to learn from him.

"Teach me your ways, oh master," I plead.

"You? Turn tricks for the rich and powerful?" Pedro frowns and gives me a once-over. Whatever impression I make has him clucking his tongue in despair. "*Dios mío*. Your hair could use a good wash for a start. Whatever this look is—" He waves disapprovingly at my denim shorts and low-cut tank top. "Might work on those cheap ass *pendejos* at the strip club, but for a man like Jaguar? Oh, honey. Your whole approach will need fine-tuning, and honestly, I'm not sure you can even pull it off."

I fake pout, though internally, I can't deny his assessment stings a little. Pedro is honest to a fault, and I know he means every word. "Am I not pretty enough, oh master?"

"No." He crosses over to me and captures my chin against his palm. With a sigh, he angles my face to better view my profile. Again, he clucks his tongue. "You aren't cunning enough. You're too desperate. I can see it all over you. A man like Jaguar gets drunk off desperation. He overdoses on it every damn day. I'm sure that whenever he walks into the club, scores of women throw themselves at him, willing to do whatever and whoever they need to get close. He'll have developed a bullshit detector even I couldn't crack. And you?" He releases me in utter exasperation and shrugs. "You wouldn't make it past the front door. You have one damning trait that even those sniveling, pathetic whores he surrounds himself with lack."

"And what is that?"

"Self-respect," he says without hesitation. "Humility. Honor. Kindness. You aren't a downright sociopath, and a man like Jaguar would see right through you. If you interest him enough, he might enjoy breaking that spirit, but in the end, you wouldn't get what you're after. Only pain and humiliation. Take my word for it. Find a new plan." Turning on his heel, he heads for my bedroom. Despite his disparaging assessment of my clothing, I bet he's eager to raid my closet to see if I have another pair of shorts. Once, he let it slip that some of his lovers enjoy roleplay.

"But if I *were* to catch his eye?" I follow him directly to my tiny closet. There he stands with his hands on his hips, inspecting the handful of items I have displayed on hangers. "How would I go about it? Don't play coy with me—I'm sure you have an idea in that twisted brain of yours. Or are you not the expert you claim to be?"

That low dig at his honor does the trick. He pivots and inspects me yet again. This time, he lingers on my thighs and the visible scars most people overlook.

"Of course, I know how," he snaps, crossing his arms while still leaving his exposed nipple in view. "But I don't think you're woman enough to try it. Hell, even I wouldn't ever attempt to mingle in the same room as Julian Domingas, let alone catch his notice."

"But...?" I inch closer, intrigued by the sly gleam in his eye. Because I know that look. It's one he sports whenever he drives by in a brand-new luxury car gifted by some mysterious big shot. Paid for in cash. "You have an idea. Spill it and let me be the judge of what I would and wouldn't do."

"You'd have to change your entire personality for one," Pedro remarks with a dismissive wave in my general direction. "You're too independent. Too bold. Men like Jaguar—those who can have anyone they want with a snap of their fingers—thrive on attaining what they seemingly can't have. But deep down, they need to know that they *can* get it eventually. One look at you and Jaguar would know that you truly had no interest in him. There is no fight."

"Are you going to beat around the bush all night, or is there a meaning to this long-winded insult of my entire personality and appearance?"

Pedro scoffs and approaches the vanity, where he keeps his stash of cigarettes for when he visits. He draws one and makes a show of lighting it with a fancy, silver lighter given to him by one of his paramours. After inhaling, he slowly exhales, blowing the smoke in my direction.

"Beat around the bush is exactly what you *can't* do when dealing with a man like Jaguar. You lay it all on the table. What you want from him. What you are willing to offer him in return."

"You said a man like him is used to women throwing themselves at him. So, I need to throw myself at him?"

He laughs. "Oh, you sweet, naïve thing. There is a difference between throwing and offering yourself on a silver platter. You pledge to give a man like that everything. Your loyalty, your body, your trust. But only to him. He must become your entire universe. Devotion is the love language to bastards like Julian Domingas. But not desperation. You position yourself as the only woman in the world who could truly give him happiness. The only woman he can trust to never betray him. Never speak of him badly, no matter what he does to you. A woman he can call his. I'm sure he's had beautiful women. Perfect women. All who have slept with another on their way up the social ladder, or who will gladly fuck or screw whoever comes after. You need to be a woman crafted solely for Julian Domingas, willing to follow him to the ends of the earth."

"So, I need to be desperate but not too desperate." I deflate, convinced I've been the butt of his elaborate joke this entire time.

Pedro doesn't laugh. "A man like Jaguar wants more than sex, Pita. More than surface-level affection or romance. He wants more than love. He craves obsession—he can't help himself. He needs a woman to see him as he sees himself. Dangerous. Perfect. Powerful. No one's fool. Can you do that? Demean yourself like that?" He cups my chin, lifting it for inspection a second time.

I don't shy from the scrutiny. "You tell me how and I will do it. For my nephew, I will do anything."

"You always were a crazy ass ride-or-die, Pita." He sighs, clucking his tongue. "I could say no, but that wouldn't stop you from going it alone."

"You know that better than anyone," I say with a sad smile. After all, we escaped Hell together, hand in hand like always.

Pedro eyes me for a long time, and I can't tell what he's thinking. Finally, he nods and gestures to the closet.

"Okay. I will bestow upon you a taste of my expertise. We will start with your hair. Then outfit. I'll pull some strings and get you something nicer than the shit you have in this junk pile. I'm sure this entire thing will blow up in your face, but you know I can't resist that pouty, doe-eyed thing you do. That will come in handy, by the way. We will need to perfect it, though. And another thing…"

"Yes?" I clasp my hands eagerly.

He props a hand on his hip, his lips pursed. "Now, this question is very important. It will determine the course of your entire harebrained scheme, so answer carefully. How do you feel about group sex?"

I try not to grimace. "I'll feel about it however you tell me to feel."

"Good answer, you kiss-ass," he says with a laugh. "From now on, you follow my every word of advice down to the letter. It's the only way you'll stay alive—trust me on that."

Trust is a piece of me only Pedro has ever earned. Enough that I don't hesitate to put my life in his hands, as well as my body.

If anyone can teach me how to seduce the most powerful man in the world, it's Pedro Juarez.

CHAPTER THREE

My journey into the world of dangerous narcos begins in an unexpected place. You can find normal men gambling at a pool hall or drooling over dancers in a strip club. Even Braulio is partial to a particular titty bar up north.

In contrast, Julian Domingas holds court in a location exclusive to him, which perfectly sets the stage for what Pedro has lovingly dubbed my suicide mission.

A fight club in West Caracass is his chosen haunt. One where ex-criminals brawl to death in an underground cage. I've heard of such matches only through the vilest rumors when it comes to the most powerful narcos. For their own amusement, they hire thugs to maim one another—when they're not buying and selling women as commodities, that is.

The fact that Pedro even knows about this place is beyond me. He didn't think to enlighten me, either. Neither did he explain where he got the red sports car I drove to this venue or who the owner of the silver business card I flash to the security guards is.

Rather than some isolated compound in the middle of nowhere, the address Pedro gave me leads to a sprawling gated complex near the upscale half of the city. The only entrance seems to be via a large garage and a set of metal double doors guarded by at least five armed men. Apparently, these events aren't open to the public. Watchful eyes track my every move, and a stern-faced man frisks me before letting me through a metal barrier.

Once inside, I find a large, square arena that slopes toward a raised fighting ring in the center. It's not quite the din of bloodshed I'd anticipated. It's...classy, almost. Black walls and gray floors create a mysterious atmosphere, and well-dressed attendants circle around with trays of champagne.

One could almost forget the enormous silver cage looming over the heart of the room. At the base of it lies a rubber mat perfect for repelling bloodstains and the like. Rows of leather chairs line four levels, each increasing in height from the main floor with steps leading down to the bottom.

Feeling out of place, I move blindly, taking everything in through a wide-eyed gaze. More people have entered, jostling beside me, and before I know it, I'm in a sea of strangers.

They aren't the ordinary crowd. In fact, they aren't even the type of people found in the strip clubs owned by the men who organize these events. Their tailored suits cast an allure typically found in some exclusive country club.

A rush of adrenaline quickens my pulse and moistens my palms with sweat. I feel as if I am stepping into a den of lions. Or, in this case, hungry jaguars.

Yet, oddly enough, the king feline is nowhere to be found.

Mingle, Pedro had warned me. *Don't get caught lurking. Force a smile and speak to any and everyone. Make an impression and seem as if any man in this arena could be your prey. In this dress, you might be able to somewhat make up for your general lack of sex appeal.*

The bastard had a point. The black, skintight one-piece he gave me stands out in this crowd for all the wrong reasons. With low-cut necklines and dangerously high skirts, most women here try to show as much skin as possible. I even receive questioning glances as I pass, but not because my dress is out-of-style.

I am a walking contradiction. This ensemble is conservative, and yet somehow *not.* Black material hugs my curves, and the design sports long sleeves that end just past my wrists. A scooped neckline teases the barest hint of cleavage and serves as the most daring attribute about me.

Basically, I look like a naughty Halloween version of a nun, sans piety.

Wearing it at all was an act of faith in Pedro's expertise. I would probably choose something red if I were to devise an outfit that would catch Jaguar's attention. Something with a slit up to my hoo-ha and a neckline equally risqué. The skimpiest clothes make men drool, after all.

Pedro's insight, however, I trust more than my own. *Stick to the script,* he warned before I left. *It sounds dramatic, Pita, but your life depends on it. This is no game.*

The impact of his words has only begun to sink in. All at once, the air becomes colder, and the room grows silent in what feels like an orchestrated moment. Then, as if on cue, an entourage of people enter the arena, and I can hear Pedro's voice whispering, *Showtime.*

I know of Julian Domingas. Everyone unfortunate enough to rub shoulders with the lower dregs of society does. Rumor and myth are the bread and butter of those in the cartels. They thrive on fear and on gravitas.

Despite the infamy, I've never seen him in person. I don't even know what he looks like. Spotting an imposing figure leading the well-dressed newcomers, I stiffen in anticipation. Could he be Julian Domingas himself? My impression of him is hard to describe.

It's not a particularly good one.

When viewed from a distance, the man more than lives up to the myth. He's beautiful but in a jagged sense. The way volcanoes can be beautiful, bathed in hot lava and spewing destruction into the world. As he approaches, my entire body tenses in ways I don't expect. It's primal. Instinctive. Also... Sexual.

I blame abstinence for that—it has been too long since I've been with anyone, let alone someone who oozes danger. Logic cannot always prevail over biology, and in this case, I'm outmatched.

Julian Domingas exudes an intensity I have never encountered before. Even Braulio lacks this specific kind of *je ne sais quoi.* He wears a black shirt with short sleeves that reveal the vivid tattoos spanning his left arm. Although he opted for dark-wash jeans instead of the expensive suit his peers prefer, he somehow seems the most regal of them all. A tribal chieftain, taking charge of a disparate arrangement of allies.

Pedro's warnings take on a new significance. My old friend was right—Jaguar is a new breed of animal. My only consolation is that most men are beasts. Monsters.

The main weakness of such a creature? Willing prey.

Trying to remember Pedro's script, I square my shoulders. According to him, I shouldn't approach Jaguar directly and throw myself at his feet as my first move. I need to mingle first, so I do, keeping to the outskirts of the crowd.

To stall for time, I inspect more of the arena. It's nicer than some movie theaters. Hell, it's nicer than my apartment building on the lower west side. The floors may be concrete, but burnished silver lighting makes the metal of the inner cage sparkle. Were we here under different circumstances, one might think this could be the stage of some elaborate abstract performance of *Cirque du Soleil.*

The purpose of this venue becomes painfully apparent as the lights dim further and the players take their places around the arena.

Violence. Pomp and circumstance. Mayhem.

Jaguar and his entourage are at the center of it all, in the seats closest to the ground floor. He has at least three women on his arm, all scantily dressed and sensually beautiful. Arm candies. Although Pedro has been laid more than I have, I immediately doubt his approach.

Confidence is a fragile thing in the world of excess money and dangerous power. From what I could garner on the grapevine, Braulio's plane leaves in exactly eight hours, and I'm no closer to stopping him. I still have to convince Jaguar to do something, should I even manage to catch his eye.

Enough worrying. I shake my head to clear it and refocus.

Inky darkness descends over the area as a puddle of illumination remains in the center. To raucous applause, two fighters take center stage, and I realize that I'm one of the few spectators who remain standing.

With trepidation, I fish the silver card from my purse and scour it for a seating number. I come up blank. Trust Pedro to skip over the finer points of masquerading as cartel property, such as where to sit at the coveted cage matches. Left with no direction, I linger on the outskirts, comforted to find that a few other people do the same, all while sipping expensive liquor from fluted glasses.

I'm dying for something to calm my frantic nerves, but refrain. That was another one of Pedro's rules. No alcohol, not even a sip.

You need your senses sharp, Pita, he warned me. *Men like Domingas don't like their women weak. Your sole focus should be on him and him alone.*

I try to embody that advice and again find myself fixated on the man in question.

Dios mío, he has a swagger few possess. He's distant and yet dominant. Unobtrusive and yet undeniable. Merely looking at him inspires a tingly, foreboding aura that makes the hair on the back of my neck stand up. As if sensing my reaction, his dark eyes flicker over the crowd, much like his namesake, hunting for prey, but never seeming to view the same woman twice.

I wait for him to spot me. Will he? It's a torturous game, and I'm always aware that time is running out. The longer I dally, the closer Francisco is to forever being trapped within his father's grasp.

But is an even worse beast truly our salvation?

Second-guessing isn't an option any longer—I'm in too deep to back down now. It's time to implement phase two. Luckily for me, Pedro's second rule was relatively straightforward. *Draw his notice. Make a scene.*

It should be easy, but my heart hammers madly in my chest, and I feel like I might puke. Perhaps that's what Pedro had in mind? Vomiting would certainly make an impression.

But no. Rather than trust my talent for the impulsive, my friend gave me explicit instructions. If only I could remember exactly... *Oh. Right.*

My fingers shake as I pull a wad of cash from my purse, more than I have ever held in my hands at once. I've seen it, of course, mainly flashed by Tiena when she used to brag about snagging a rich catch like Braulio.

I had never been so lucky—or perhaps so fortunate—to have a man pay my way so frivolously. Pedro, lovingly, doesn't count in this instance, though for tonight, he's supplied me with enough assets to make up my old salary at least ten times over.

And as for the last man in my past... I was the one who paid a debt to him in blood and pain.

Not now, a part of me warns, banishing the memory. *Focus only on Jaguar.*

Holding the money clip securely, I descend the wide steps leading to the cage. The fighting hasn't begun yet, and the beefy fighters circle each other while I attempt to ignore the display entirely. If I can make it through this night without seeing a drop of blood, it will be one small win after weeks of heartache. Given the man I'm after, it's a selfish wish, but I'm pathetic enough to pin my hopes on it.

With a determined inhale, I arrange my expression the way Pedro taught me and keep my eyes focused straight ahead— not on the predator I'm poised to walk right past.

A certain moment can remain etched in your mind forever. The smells. The sights. The sounds. One day I'll recollect these tense few seconds with the painful reverence of battle scars.

He doesn't look at me, Julian Domingas, but the fact doesn't panic me. It intrigues me. To him, I don't even deserve a glance, and I tremble at the thought of what it would take to grab his full attention. Far more than a party dress and a bold stunt.

Dios mío, I hope Pedro knows what he's doing.

During my internal struggle, a man in a black suit stepped into the ring, and a hushed silence falls. In fluent Spanish, he details an exciting spectacle planned for the evening. Then he coyly asks the crowd if there are any bets to be had.

At least Pedro warned me about this part of the game in advance. Not only do they take glee in watching these poor bastards pummel each other. They also place bets on the carnage. In the end, whoever survives, or gets less maimed, wins. In higher-stakes fights, the spectators even trade statistics and shit, but the main point is, whatever choice you make, you do it with flair. Bravado.

You are a woman who knows what she wants, Pedro insisted. *Make sure the entire arena knows it.*

When the man calls for bets, several patrons raise their hands, flashing bills to back up their boasts.

A grand here. Two grand there. Ten grand on the noticeably bigger of the two fighters.

It can't hurt to ignore one small bit of Pedro's advice. Rather than make my choice at random, I take the time to inspect the men in question. One fighter draws the lion's share of excitement, and he holds himself assuredly with confidence most are betting their money on.

The other fighter is lankier, his muscles less proportioned. At first glance, he doesn't look like much, but I recognize his stocky build for its quiet lethality.

Raising my hand, I murmur a number that would make me choke in any other instance and point to the fighter I aim to support.

Nearly every head in the arena swivels in my direction. Most of them are laughing, with females looking at me in amused contemplation while their masters chuckle with delight. Such a silly woman I must be, let her off her leash to play with the money no doubt given to her by a doting lover. Where is he, this powerful man? Nowhere to be seen, and I make a show of standing in the aisle alone, money in hand.

Even the MC chuckles. "Well, the chica has balls you can't deny." He humors me with a playful wink before scanning the crowd for more bids. Not even a minute later, a woman approaches with a silver tray and quietly gestures that I place my bid onto it. Once I do, she skirts off, while the MC continues his hunt for fresh offerings. Suddenly, he pauses, and his eyes widen.

Then I hear a voice behind me, cold and chilling.

"I'll double her bet, but for the other fighter."

Above my frantically racing heartbeat, I can almost hear Pedro smugly telling me, *See Pita? I was right. You have him hooked—now carefully reel him in, but remember to play the game.*

Slowly, I turn as if innocently hunting for the figure who could have made such a scandalous boast. Someone with such authority to have the entire room erupt with gasps of excited glee.

My search doesn't last long—he's looking directly at me. *Dios mío,* his eyes. A shade of brown with an undercurrent of orange, they gleam like nothing I've ever seen. They enhance the golden hue of his skin and contrast with a head of short dark brown hair. Faced with him head-on, I'm reminded of the creature he proudly displays on his left bicep. Even the tattoo is impressive up close—an intricate black feline peeks out from behind a swath of leaves in deep indigos and subtle greens.

The tattooed jaguar's teeth are bared, but the man has his mouth closed, his lips quirking in a smirk that cannot be read. One of amusement? Pity? Contemplation? A tendril of alarm runs down my spine with every new guess. With a face that is harder to gauge than Braulio's, he makes me feel blind. At any other time, that alone would make me doubt this scheme. In another universe, perhaps, where Francisco isn't at risk and my life has a much more optimistic trajectory. I've witnessed secondhand what happens to those who play with fire by ingratiating themselves with the cartel.

Hell unfolds, and those left alive in the aftermath are forever scarred by it.

In spite of his role, Julian Domingas is a deceptively handsome arsonist. His eyes rake over me with lazy, hungry ease, making me feel stripped naked despite my conservative ensemble. His lips quirk further. Then part, allowing a pink tongue to slither between them. Apparently, he likes what he sees, enough to beckon me with a wave of his hand.

Commanded, I smile as a woman should in such a situation. Internally, I'm shitting myself. Dear old Pedro seemed highly skeptical I would even get this far. After all, a man with everything or anyone in the world should have no use for a woman like me. *In theory,* Pedro added with an apologetic frown. *You're hot, Pita, but averagely so. These days women have more ass and tits than they know what to do with. In fact, I hope you don't get noticed by Jaguar's type. They get their hooks into you, Pita, and there is no going back.*

He had a point.

The feeling ripping through me right now is reminiscent of a barbed hook sinking into my chest. I'm a helpless, cornered fish being slowly reeled in by a fisherman with unclear motives. Will he grow bored of me and toss me back out? Or will he save me for dinner?

There's nothing more disgusting than how desperately I want him to pick the second option. Only now am I one-hundred percent sure of this insane plan—if any man could bring Braulio to his knees, it is this one. I sense his power like some can detect a change in the weather. There is a certain taste in the air that heralds one hell of a storm on the horizon.

I want to master that chaos.

Even as a wave of apprehension worms its way through my chest, my smile widens with renewed resolve. It's now or never, and as I start forward, all I see for a moment is Francisco's face. I can't even imagine what he's been through after a month spent with that asshole. Tiena was a mess, but even she had noticed the bruises.

I'll step in next time, she lied more than once. *I promise, Lupe. It's not that big a deal. If I push him too far, he'll do more than just pop him in the mouth. Do you want that? Do you want to see Franco in the hospital?*

Like a fool, I'd kept my mouth shut, and in return, my sister vanished. Has Braulio killed her? I don't even have the mental bandwidth to consider it. My sister had become a stranger to me by then, more concerned with her money and expensive clothing than her own damn son.

The grim truth is too twisted that I've never voiced it to anyone, not even Pedro. But… I hope she's dead. It would mean that she got in the way, at least. Spoke up to him. Said something to defend Francisco and paid for it with the ultimate sacrifice any mother should be willing to make.

But I know Tiena and selfless martyrdom was never her style. It's far more likely that she cut and ran of her own volition. That she willingly left Franco behind.

God, it hurts to think of her. While Braulio is a worthy opponent of my hate, she was once the only other person in the world I could trust besides myself. It took me twenty-eight damn years to realize how naïve that had been.

Ironically, Tiena is the reason I withdrew from the cruel circus she referred to as "polite society." A sea of peons wrapped around Braulio's thumb, eager to fuck, lie, cheat, and do whatever at his whim. She fooled herself, living behind that fantasy, but I always saw right through it.

To his credit, or perhaps not, the man looking into my eyes is more than some pompous ringleader. Those in his orbit aren't reduced to circus performers whose only responsibility is to entertain him. No. Even the women on his arm sport the same panicked look in their eyes as I approach.

They are rabbits in a cage, preening for the predator's discretion. I shouldn't… But I think I find comfort in that. Morbid, cold, finite comfort. Braulio torments those who displease him.

Jaguar? I get the sense he doesn't bother with mind games. He kills those who dare to get in his way and probably does it with the muscular hands braced on his knees. As if aware of my gaze, he flexes them one by one, taking care to loudly crack each knuckle.

Without a word, a half-naked blond and two brunettes scramble from him onto seats in the next row.

He must reel in new fish often.

"That's a big bet for such a small woman." His voice—I react to it first. A sinfully deep baritone, penetrating my skin to the muscle beneath. Oddly enough, I can't tell if it's attractive. My belly doesn't quake, and I don't instantly imagine what he would sound like murmuring into my ear during pillow talk.

There is a measured quality to his tone few men use. As if every word is a test meant to gauge how I will respond. Think. Act. To pair with the assessment, his gaze slides over me a second time, lingering over what little skin my dress does show—namely my legs.

I'm so distracted by his scrutiny that I slip up. Rather than the carefully rehearsed laugh Pedro insisted upon, I improvise. A quip slips out unchallenged.

"If size was all that mattered, I think half of the human population would be left very, very lonely."

Shit. I stiffen as those dark eyes narrow. Then he laughs, but in a harsh, quick way as if he didn't intend to. His eyes sparkle as though I've passed some unspoken test.

"Fair enough. Come here." He extends his hand, and I take it without thinking, expecting gentle gallantry. Pedro warned me his regulars loved to kiss his fingers, making a show of their flattery.

Jaguar grips me hard. I gasp as he wrenches me forward, onto his thigh. I'm left with my back to him, and my head cocked at an awkward angle.

"What's your name?" he asks, settling one of those massive hands over my knee.

Again, shock robs me of my script. I blurt out, "You can call me Lupe—"

"I didn't ask what I *could* call you." He still holds my hand and squeezes it so hard I bite my lip to silence a groan. "I asked *what your name is.*"

Think, Lupe! Anger on him has a smell. A flavor I can taste on my tongue, mingling with the faint scents of cologne, alcohol, and fresh blood wafting from the ring. It's fiery and sharp enough to know that I never want to experience it in full.

So, again, I improvise. One thing Pedro said keeps echoing in my head—*how do you catch a man who can have anyone? You be the only one. The only one who could ever satisfy him. Crave him. Please him. You want this man above all else, and that's the difference.*

"I meant that *you* can call me Lupe," I purr, lowering my voice the way Tiena would when chatting up her next mark. A slight tremor undermines the sensuality, but I ignore it and crane my neck to face him head-on. Jesus Christ, those eyes. Even as they pierce through me, I soldier on. "Not many people can. It has special meaning to me, far better than Lupita." I extend my hand and widen my grin as quiet calculation flits across those fathomless eyes. "Sanchez. At your service."

"Lupita." I shiver at how his tongue seems to catch over the syllables, mangling them into something indecipherable. In the language of jaguars, my name is a series of growled notes and grated inflection. "I'm sure you already know who I am."

It isn't a question, and I don't know how to answer. Pedro's script is in the wind, and I'm scrambling to recall snatches of his advice. Something about confidence. Calm.

"I know *of* you," I admit, turning back to the match. Sometime amid this strange conversation, the fighting began, and I instantly tear my gaze away again. In the process, I find myself staring at a couple sitting a few seats over. They pretend to be engaged in the fighting, but the reality is they can't seem to take their eyes off my direction. In fact, most people in the nearby vicinity seem to be staring this way.

Because of Jaguar and how easily he dominates a room. I can tell he thrives off the attention, and yet in the same breath, he doesn't seem to notice. He's a top-tier predator who takes his ability to intimidate for granted. That could come in handy. I try to remember it.

"You're a powerful man, Julian Domingas," I add, risking another glance at him. "Only a fool would be unaware of your reputation."

He smiles in a fleeting, terrifying way. It's so quick, like a lightning strike, and just as devastating. My belly quivers, and I'm not sure if it's due to fear or arousal. Chilling reputation and handsomeness aside, his body is built for domination. Muscles carved from stone press against my ass, thighs, and back. It makes me shudder to think what it would feel like to be beneath him. I don't know if the picture unfolding in my mind is sexy or horrifying.

"Powerful," he echoes, demanding my sole focus once more. "Go on."

It isn't a harmless bit of flirting, and even I have enough sense to stiffen at the carefully concealed warning. Men so high in this shadowy realm are always on guard, well aware anyone stupid enough to approach them does so only to ask for something. Nothing else.

Pedro did warn me, and in this instance, I clearly remember his advice down to the letter.

"I have a proposition for you," I say, cutting to the chase while making my honesty apparent. "In fact, I believe you are the only man in the world who can help me."

A brown eyebrow quirks up, and I pray I have his interest.

"Is that so?" His palm rubs up and down from my hip to my thigh, sending a jolt through my system. "And what is that?"

I'm not fooled by his playful tone. His eyes are shrouded in shadow from this angle, and amid the backdrop of flesh striking flesh, I feel the gravity of a pious parishioner asking the devil for a favor.

Is my soul worth the risk?

Standing at the gates of Hell, it's far too late to turn back.

"I want you to help me," I say, letting genuine desperation leech into my voice. "I believe you are the only one who can."

His hand stills, and his eyelids lower a fraction. The hairs on the back of my neck stand on end.

"Is that so?" His eyes flick over me and return to the fight. I don't dare follow, so I have no clue who's winning, or the cause of the pained groans that erupt from the crowd next. I can't take my eyes off him, sensing that I'm dangerously close to failing some unspoken test. Just like that, I've bored him.

How to get his attention back? How?

"There are other men I could have gone to," I add, hating how a stutter creeps into my words. Pedro warned me against begging, but I can't help it. I am. "Luis Romanos. Leo Corleon—"

"You have interesting taste in men," he chides. His eyes don't budge from their current fixation, but his hand strokes me again as if to encourage me to continue.

So, I do. Those are men cut from the same cloth as Braulio, capable of overtaking him, but they never gave me the time of day. Perhaps another tidbit of the truth is called for here?

"They lack what I need," I go on, speaking above a pained groan that comes from the direction of the arena. At the back of my mind, some moral, logical part of me screams that I'm just feet away from a man most likely breathing his last breath. I've gotten good at pushing down that voice over the years.

"I need someone who won't be held back by moral constraints or fear. I need someone ruthless."

"You need to explain what the fuck it is you want without the flowery language." He pulls his hand from me and inclines his head as if to banish me. One small fact keeps me rooted in place—I recognize that the action could double as an impatient cue to speak.

"Not here," I say, with a wary glance around. Braulio is nowhere near Jaguar's status, but he still has his allies. I'm sure a few of them are here tonight, wondering why I look so similar to his past side piece. I can't take the risk of word getting back to him. "We can discuss it after the fight. I'll make the conversation more than worth your while."

Pedro warned that I would need to sell that line. Say it with a straight face and as though I meant every word to drip with innuendo. In practice, my voice shakes, robbing my tone of any sensuality or flirtation.

The truth is, up this close, there is no way in hell I could sleep with this man. In the lead-up to this point, I told myself I would do anything, but even reckless bravery won't help me here.

Jaguar seems interested in something far more intense than fucking. Something dangerous and violent that I might not survive unscathed. Sex with him would be entering a jungle unguarded against the predator lurking inside it. I may be desperate, but I'm not suicidal.

Yet.

Though it seems I misjudged him. His expression remained disinterested until my voice cracked over "while." The proposition didn't intrigue him. My unease does.

He flicks those eyes in my direction, and my heart skips a beat.

"After," he murmurs, but I can't tell from his tone if that's a good sign or bad. No one has ever put my people-reading skills to the test like this. Every interaction feels like a game of roulette. Throwing me for another loop, he inclines his head. "You seem to be one lucky woman."

"Huh?" I don't understand what he means until a round of deafening cheers go up from the crowd around us. Though, on second appraisal, most of those "cheers" seem to be groans of disappointment. The fight must be over, and as I finally turn to the cage, the MC stands there, holding up the winner's bloodied fist.

Sporting a swollen nose and a nasty bruised eye, the eventual winner isn't the beefy fighter who drew the lion's share of bets. He is the man I picked, looking none too worse for wear as his opponent lies motionless behind him. I won, but the full significance of the moment doesn't sink in until a guttural voice croons against my ear, "It seems the little wolf has won the lion's share."

Won. More money than I even know what to do with—though technically, it's all Pedro's.

"Smart girl to get me on your side before taking my money," Jaguar adds with a low, deceptively playful laugh. "Smart girl. Where to next?"

My mind is reeling. I can't recall Pedro's script fast enough, but it seems Jaguar doesn't intend to wait for an answer.

As if on cue, he snaps his fingers, and his entourage stands and begins to file from the arena.

"Come." He rises from his chair and inclines his head toward me, but captures my hand in that punishing grip. I'm tethered to his side with little room to maneuver, forced to keep up with his long, quick strides. He's about a foot taller than me, and I hate how small I feel against his bulk. Fragile.

The curious glances of those we pass don't help. They don't seem jealous or even mildly interested. They seem… relieved, especially the women.

What have I gotten myself into?

I feel the need to slow down. Breathe.

"Shouldn't I collect my winnings first?" I manage to ask.

He chuckles without looking my way. "They'll credit it to your account, baby. You don't come here often, do you?"

I say nothing, risking silence over the truth or a lie. Pedro didn't prepare me for that question. In fact, he gave me little coaching on what to do outside of the basics. Though, his advice has gotten me this far, so I can't complain too much. Besides, I'm not here for the money.

As Jaguar takes me from the arena to what looks like an underground garage, I pay closer attention to the people around us. His three-piece ensemble of women lurks near his left side, their lips pouty—though again, I get the sense their displeasure is merely an act. It's both a relief and a terrifying feeling to not be the object of his attention.

Even Tiena tolerated Braulio with simpering smiles and the smugness of a cat that got the mouse whenever he took her out on his arm. When he grew bored of her—and those moments came and went like clockwork—she would seethe in paranoid agony. *What will I do if he throws me away?*

What she should have been asking is, what will happen to Francisco? To me? How will we pick up the pieces she so carelessly left behind?

Some might pity my sister. I don't.

"You do this a lot." Jaguar's guttural murmur snaps me back to reality with the force of a blow. He isn't angry—yet. But I suspect he's inching there, eyeing me with an eyebrow cocked, his eyelids lowered to slice those piercing irises in half.

"W-What?" I ask, genuinely confused.

As if warning me, he squeezes my hand. *Don't question.*

"Seem distracted around a man you've worked so damn hard to draw the notice of," he adds.

Oh. A wave of stiffness runs through my body, and my heart falls to the floor. How much does he know? His face is blank, and I feel like I have been thrown onto a fragile sheet of glass. It only takes one wrong move for everything to shatter.

Luckily, an abrupt change of scenery provides a much-needed distraction. We've approached a large, luxury SUV that I presume to be his. A man steps forward and opens the door, but Jaguar grips it and nods his head in a way I assume dismisses the others.

"I ride alone. Miss Lupe and I need to continue our discussion in private."

Dios mío. Is this a good sign? Bad? Too much about this man unnerves me. As he adjusts his grip on my hand, I feel my stomach twist.

"After you."

I sit on a spacious leather seat, and he slides in beside me. With a mirrored table and what looks like a mini bar, the back of this vehicle is designed to entertain.

"Alright. I've let you play your game," Jaguar taunts as the driver closes the door, plunging us in darkness. "Now cut to the chase, *chica.* What do you want?"

"Protection," I say. Pedro stressed the importance of that—no bullshit—but even if he hadn't, I doubt I'd be tempted to lie anyway. Deceit seems to be a very dangerous game to play with a man like this.

Honesty may be equally foolish, but at least I don't have to think so hard to stay one step ahead.

"I need your help," I add, tilting my head to take him in. Bathed in shadow and the artificial glow of the garage that pierces the tinted windows, he's a specter of darkness. The literal devil himself, or perhaps something far more unpredictable. A hungry jaguar.

"Keep talking." His voice has that dangerous tone again.

I rush to speak. "His name is Braulio—"

"Rivera," Jaguar fills in. "I've heard of the man."

I choke out a sigh. Is this relief flooding my veins? I don't know. His tone is neutral, though I highly doubt he's one of Braulio's allies. No, in fact, I know they aren't fond of each other in the slightest. In recent years, Braulio has become increasingly hungry for power. He'd stab his own mother for a bigger slice of the city, and Jaguar doesn't strike me as the friendly type.

"He's dangerous," I blurt, forgetting my script. Hell, fuck the polished, rehearsed spiel Pedro had me devise. "I want him out of commission, and it needs to happen soon. Before—"

I break off, though he never says a word. He is angry, his attention is waning. One of his thumbs strokes the wrist bones of my captive hand, but it is a caress that is far from gentle or loving. It's the way a lumberjack might test a piece of wood before taking the initial swing with an ax.

"You have an awfully big enemy, chica. Did he fuck another bitch on you? Kill your lover?"

The game has shifted again. I've gone from entertaining him to boring him. Though, should I be that surprised? After all, how many women has he had come crawling to him in the name of revenge?

My tongue is tingling from fear, but there is no turning back. I hunt for his gaze in the darkness and hold it. One second. Two. After I'm certain he's seen the serious gleam in my eyes, I continue.

"He has my son."

I'm surprised by how gritty the words sound. In a way, it doesn't seem like a lie at all. Maybe it isn't. I love Francisco *more* than if he were my own. With Tiena for a mother, he needs all the love and then some.

My fear for him keeps me calm long after Jaguar has let go of my hand and turned his focus to the window. We've left the garage, driving down some darkened street. I should be worried about our eventual destination, but I can't be.

A mere taste of Jaguar's disapproval crumbles my carefully rehearsed ruse, and I become the desperate, pathetic Lupita Sanchez Pedro warned me not to be.

"He's taking him out of the country tonight," I say. "I have to stop him. I can't let… He's hurting him, Franco. I don't want him dead, but I want—"

"You think you can come to me with your petty battles and bullshit?"

Ice runs through my veins, and for a second, I stop breathing. I stop thinking. Instinct is my only tether, and I manage to choke out, "It's not petty—"

"You want me to start a war with Braulio Rivera on the word of some side bitch who wants her brat back?"

He doesn't laugh, but his mockery doesn't sting any less. I'm grateful that I can't see his face clearly. Grateful that he can't see mine. Tears prickle behind my eyes, and I know they'll fall eventually.

The irony is that I never cry in pain. If I did that, I wouldn't have any tears left by now. No, I cry when bitches like Tiena abandon their children with no warning. I cry when cruel men humiliate me in public for the world to see. I cry when I hate so much it spills out of me in liquid form, and there is no stopping the tempest.

But Jaguar doesn't know that. A swath of light illuminates his features, and from the smirk on his face, I assume he sees my glistening eyes as weakness.

"I want you to go to war because that's what men like you do," I counter bitterly. From the back of my mind, I hear a voice suspiciously like Pedro's warning me of the danger of acting recklessly. Impulsively. Running my mouth around a man like Domingas could get me killed.

His eyes predictably darken, but I do not feel afraid. *So be it.* I'd rather die giving it my all than curl in a ball and accept defeat. *Damn the consequences.* Reaching for his hand through the darkness, I squeeze the hard, lethal bits of muscle and bone. Caressing them beneath my thumb, I endure the low, questioning sound that escapes his throat.

"You destroy those weaker," I tell him. "That is what I want. What I need."

"And what would be in it for me?" He turns the tables, crushing my fingers in a brutal grasp. *Damn it.* I cry out, and squeeze my eyes shut. For a second, Jaguar disappears, replaced by a figure I refuse to remember.

Do you think you can challenge me, little butterfly? he would growl. *Think again. Unless you think you have the balls to...*

No! I shake my head to banish the memory and wrench my eyes open. Not now. He can't hurt me here.

And the pain inflicted by Jaguar... I can survive it. Pursing my lips, I breathe through it and force myself to face him.

Darkness once again obscures his expression, and I can't make out a single detail. Only his voice provides a clue as to his thought process. Cold, simmering apathy.

"I don't need your money, chica. And if you're on the run from Braulio, I doubt you have a damn thing to your name. Nothing in this world comes without an expectation of repayment."

The sudden switch to business terms sends me reeling. So, this is the real difference between kings and those who play pretend. Thugs desperate to rise in the ranks rely on violence and fear to pave their path up the pecking order. Braulio excels in it and doesn't waste his time on pretty words or complex thinking. He's a mindless dog chasing a bone.

Jaguar is different, and that…unnerves me? Excites me, even. This will be a challenge—far more involved than flashing my tits and relying on seduction. He isn't a mindless brute who utilizes his fists to get what he wants. It's chess—not checkers—he's playing.

My only useful course of action here would be to prove myself more than a worthless pawn. But how?

"I'm not offering you money, Jaguar."

He laughs. "Oh, I can see that. You think I didn't notice that the card you entered with wasn't tied to your name?"

My cheeks flush. When had he even been able to see it? I'd been by his side for most of the match. Unless…

He'd done so well before I even placed a bet. Pedro knows his shit, after all—I'd gotten his notice long before I realized it.

"You pretend well enough, but you aren't from these parts," he continues, his voice low. "Your old master kept you on a tight leash. To the point that you jump at any man who looks at you. Lawrence Bailey must be one hell of a man, so confident in his woman to let you go out alone."

That must be the name of the card's owner. Misogyny aside, I'm stunned to realize how much he's learned in such a short time. Bless Pedro's soul that he prepared me for this instance.

"I belong to no one. My friend procured a way for me to attend tonight's event. I don't even know the man whose card I used."

Does he believe that? Damn this lighting. I still can't tell. He has his face angled away from me though, and his thumb is steadily caressing my wrist with increasing frequency.

"Ah, but you belong to Braulio, don't you," he surmises. "I don't pick over leftovers. You are sexy in that little nun getup—I will give you that. Strolling around with that hair in a pious little bun. You certainly know how to play your part."

"I was never Braulio's," I insist. "But I can be *yours*. You asked what I offer. It's me."

He scoffs, and my plan derails for the umpteenth time. This man. He's so damn unpredictable. For a second—just one —I regret ever coming here. My time would be much better spent casing every mansion Braulio owns, praying to find some way to get to Franco before it's too late.

The thought of him being shoved onto a plane and headed for God knows where breaks my heart to pieces. Nothing this man could inflict on me could ever come close.

"You?" We're on a well-lit street, and a passing streetlamp provides the illumination necessary to make out his eyes. And that stern mouth, fixated in a frown. "Don't take this as an insult, but I could have any woman I want. You've seen the three I have now. What makes you different?"

"Because I offer you more than just sex or a casual lay," I say, brandishing my chin toward him. "I offer me. My loyalty. My obedience. My honesty. I could be a bigger asset to you than I think you realize. Let me serve you, and I will never forsake your protection."

"And you are so special? I don't think so." He releases my hand and strokes his chin while leaning back into his seat. "Even if I did agree to extend my help. Would you scamper to the next man the second I threw you aside?"

Pedro warned me this could happen. *You can't back down,* he told me. *You alone have just not what he wants, but what he needs. Don't back down without proving that.*

That only brings up a very good question—What does Jaguar need?

"A man like you could have any woman he wants," I begin, "but one who will screw you and then chase after another leader in the cartel when she wants a new purse or new shoes. I am not so easily swayed. I want a powerful man who will never fall from his throne. I believe that could be you. No. *Is* you. Your trio of women can offer you a good time for a night or two. I'm offering you more than that."

"Believe me, chica. No one's pussy is that good." His laugh is guttural, bordering on a growl. At least he's honest, openly conveying his thoughts of my little spiel.

I'm failing.

"More than pussy is what is on the table," I rasp, laying out every insane, obscure aspect of this plan imaginable. What could he want that no one else could provide? A fantasy that no one on earth could resist. Not even me.

"I can understand you," I say. "I will never want more from you than what you can give. I offer you unwavering fealty that will never break. Do your research on me, if you must. I welcome it. I am not leftovers, as you put it. I only go after men I know are worthy of me."

"You talk a good game—I'll give you that." His laughter is richer than ever, but deeper too. It cuts me to the bone, resonating in parts of my body I didn't even know existed. In the face of his laser-like gaze, I stiffen, paralyzed.

"But I'm not interested in your soul. You've intrigued me this far, so I will humor you. What would fucking with Rivera, a man who owns a majority share of the outlying territory, do for me? I control far more, and to be honest with you, he isn't even on my radar. Keeping him around does me more good than not."

It's what I feared, though I shoot down the logical voice in my head insisting upon that very thing. Strategically, Braulio played his cards well. While, if given a chance, he would gun for Jaguar's position in a heartbeat, even he knew when to lie low and obey the status quo. Knowing the man, I refuse to attribute his caution to cunning or strategy. Mere cowardice is what holds him back.

"You think your pretty little words and sexy little dress are enough to convince me to rock the boat?" Jaguar wonders. "Frankly, Lupe, I can't tell if you're that brave or that damn naïve."

The truth is probably a bit of both.

"A man in your position must know that the most dangerous threats are the ones you can't see," I point out.

He cocks his head further. "Are you telling me that Braulio Rivera is gunning to make a move against me?"

I hesitate. Do I want to potentially get Braulio killed? The answer is simple—*no*. But if I need leverage, his welfare certainly won't get in my way—especially when I recall Franco's bruises. Never mind. I'd love to see the bastard bleed.

"Who wouldn't want to be the most powerful man this side of the country?" I counter. "I think many men wouldn't hesitate to do whatever it takes to unseat you."

"Is that a threat?"

I have enough sense to visibly shiver at the insinuation.

"It's the truth," I rasp, painfully aware of just how close he is. His scent is a strange mixture of cigar smoke, alcohol, and something indiscernible. A salty scent reminiscent of seawater. Or... Blood? "I don't think it should be an insult to state as much."

"Not an insult," he murmurs in a mocking tone that raises more goosebumps over my tender flesh. "But a death wish, perhaps? I wonder... If I were to reach out to Rivera and mention our little conversation, what would he say?"

"Do it." *Damn.* That wasn't part of Pedro's script, but I can't resist the part of me emboldened by the taunt. If he contacted Braulio and lured him out into the open, I could get a read on the bastard's location. Then I could somehow contact Pedro and beg him to use his contacts to rescue Francisco. Then I could…

"Eyes on me," Jaguar warns.

My shivers become full-blown tremors. The effect this man has on me… It's violent, and I don't know how far to let it go unchallenged.

When I obey his command, he watches me with renewed interest. I'm not sure what, but something has changed his mind—or gotten him to listen more closely, at least. Good.

"I told you why I came to you," I continue before he can speak. "Do what you must, but the man I've heard rumors about doesn't seem like the type to balk at a challenge. You keep Braulio here in the city, and you will see just what a threat he presents."

"And again, I ask what you plan to offer for a trade." His tongue shoots out to graze his lower lip as his eyes rake me over from head to toe.

The car has stopped, I realize. We're near a puddle of light bright enough to cast his features into stark focus. God, he's beautiful. Alone with him, there is no denying that, but I can feel the tension coiled in his body from here. I know exactly what "bargain" he has in mind, and it's more terrifying to broach than I thought going into this.

After years of abstinence, this isn't how I imagined dipping back into the world of intimacy.

"No trade," I say, struggling to recall Pedro's advice. *Men like that? They want to believe you're interested in more than money. More than their power. Sell them that fantasy, and they'll give you the whole damn world.*

Luckily, I don't need the world. I just need Francisco safe. I need that monster away from my family, and, depending on how my mood goes, I need to find answers about what really happened to Tiena.

"You do what is merely in your nature, and I will give you my loyalty. Everything. But it won't be a trade."

"Such pretty words from such a sexy little mouth," Jaguar growls. "Some men might be tempted to test how far you'll go to back up that promise."

He opens the door on his end and climbs out of the vehicle, leaving me to follow. He doesn't extend his hand or offer me any assistance, regulating me once again to a plaything he's merely toying with. His moods are so volatile and hard to get a grasp on.

Already paces away, he walks at a speed I sprint to keep up with, risking my balance in Pedro's borrowed high heels. When I finally take stock of our surroundings, my belly dips ominously. I'm used to luxury after lurking on the periphery of Braulio's influence.

Never have I seen a mansion of this opulence up close.

The man must bathe in money, but the sprawling, modern-style architecture and the decadent fountains lining the entrance aren't what thrill me. The windows do. So many large, gleaming windows that reveal swaths of the dwelling's interior.

An abundance of glass signifies the confidence of a man who does not feel the need to hide behind high walls or hired muscle. He taunts those against him to line up their shot and take it. If they have the balls to.

As I follow him inside, my heart skips another beat. A pristine foyer lined in gold-flecked marble paves the way deeper inside, but Jaguar doesn't take me on a tour. Instead, he heads up a winding staircase and into what seems to be a personal billiard room overlooking an illuminated outdoor pool where several scantily-clad women mill about in the water. I'm not threatened by them.

What I find waiting for me on the leather couches and leaning against the massive pool table in the center of the room, however, terrifies me.

CHAPTER FOUR

At least ten men fixate in my direction. With every passing second, my alarm grows. They eye me the way Francisco would the jelly donuts I'd bring him during our visits. Like a child promised a tantalizing treat.

To cement my unease, Jaguar stalks forward to claim the spotlight, his teeth bared in a feral grin. Although I am not too familiar with his emotions, I recognize danger when I see it. With his eyes flashing, he ticks every box in the potential hazard category.

"You want to earn my help, chica?" he asks. "Then show my friends and me here just how badly you want it."

Shit. Panic robs me of all my senses, and I stumble back on my heels, seconds from bolting altogether. I don't know why I'm surprised whenever men reveal their true colors. Of course, Jaguar is no different than the rest, lording his power over those much weaker.

The sad part? I would easily fall into his trap if I didn't know better. Desperation would urge me to let these men do whatever they wanted to. I'd tell myself I had no choice. No hope. Sometimes, when I'm feeling charitable, I like to think that's how Tiena felt before crawling to Braulio on her hands and knees, her honor and pride be damned.

It's a lie, of course. Tiena was never alone—she always had me.

And I still have Pedro. His words come to me now, and I say them with all the conviction I can muster. In reality, it's just one simple phrase. "No."

"No?" Jaguar laughs in a slow, menacing way. His eyes seem to darken to a lethal hue, verging on black. "But I thought you wanted my help so badly."

"I do," I admit, lifting my chin to better hold that penetrating stare. A part of me wails that I'm blowing my only chance, and I should shut up and commit to the reckless danger I signed up for.

But after meeting Jaguar in person, I think Pedro was right in one assessment. He is nothing if not prideful—and selfish.

Fortunately for me, I know exactly how to stroke such an ego. "Do you really think I'd insult you by debasing myself at the first opportunity? Any woman worthy of you would never sink so low."

More importantly, such a woman would lose his respect forever.

"Oh?" His eyelids lower a fraction—something I'm beginning to find happens when he's thinking. Or when he's caught off guard. Emboldened by the reaction, I take a single step forward, my eyes on him.

"I respect you far too much to ever insult you like that, Jaguar."

"Insult me?" He strokes his chin and levels me with another searing glance. "Oh no, Lupe. You putting on this bullshit act is what insults me." His free hand clenches into a fist. "You know what I do like? Women who shut their mouths and obey. You want my help, Lupe? I've just named my price. Show us all a very good time, and I'll consider your request."

Bastard. I can't help the anger that rips through me, white-hot. Instantly, part of his aloof veneer vanishes. He isn't all-powerful and armed with dangerous cunning. He's a ruthless sadist, just like Braulio. Just like…

Diego.

My blood runs cold at the observation. It's been so long since I've dared to think of his name. The fact that I am now must be a warning sign from my subconscious, and I rush to heed it. Turning on my heel, I head blindly for the door.

And I make my first major mistake of the night.

"Where the hell do you think you're going?" Jaguar's tone teleports me a decade into the past. I'd been on the verge of seventeen then, so enamored with an older man I'd given him everything. My body. My soul. My sanity.

Only to have him throw it all in my face and mockingly demand, "*Where the hell do you think you're going, butterfly?*" He meant it as an opened-ended question. By that point, I had no one to run to but him.

Not anymore. Diego is gone, and I am no longer that frightened little girl.

Despite Pedro's warnings and any hope of saving Franco this way, my response to Jaguar is instinctual and driven by rage. "I'm going to find someone man enough to do the job."

With his beautiful gowns and nip slips, Pedro is a more promising option than a psychopathic narco, anyway. If I beg hard enough, he might be able to pull some strings despite his prior insistence. It's my only option.

"Wait. I said wait—*stop*, Lupe."

With each terse word, my entire body resonates with the authority laced within that lethal tone. I do stop. When I look back, Jaguar hasn't budged from his position, but his entire stance has changed, transforming him from a playful bachelor into a formidable opponent. Only a woman with a death wish would deny someone so powerful.

"You think you can dictate to me?" he asks, his head cocked, face in shadow.

I should be afraid, but it's somehow easier than ever to ignore my trembling limbs and nod. "I would never insult you," I counter. "But if you would rather test me, I don't have the time. I told you what I offer. Take it or leave it."

His men erupt in taunting laughter that dies when their leader doesn't join in.

"A woman who wants to *honor* me would do whatever the hell I say," Jaguar says, parroting my voice with a guttural note. "You'd sleep with one man or a thousand, merely to please me."

Damn it. He's a narcissist too, it seems—a potential snag Pedro had warned me about. *Some men are fucking psychos, Pita. If he doesn't take no for an answer, you run like hell.*

"I wouldn't want to deny you what you deserve," I tell him, surprised by how strongly my voice resonates. "What I can offer, is for you alone and no one else. Yours. Compelling me to perform in a charade would sully that. Ruin it. You would never know how good it would be to have me all to yourself."

More laughter echoes throughout the room. Can I even blame them? I don't recognize the words coming out of my mouth. Tiena, at her most desperate, would never make such a boast. She fucked Braulio within minutes of meeting him and did so in full view of his boys merely to impress him. I know because she told me, her eyes wide with excitement as if that was something to be proud of. *I proved my loyalty to him, Pita...*

When Jaguar says nothing, I'm sure I have my answer. Loyalty with him is transactional as well. Heavy with defeat,

I head for the hall, already switching gears toward a last-ditch effort. Pedro. His cartel contacts. If they won't help, I'll somehow find a way to hijack a private airplane if I have to.

In a daze, I head for that spiral staircase, and I'm caught off guard by the grip that comes from nowhere to cinch my wrist. A brutal motion wrenches me backward, and I spin around to find Jaguar leading me down the hall toward that billiard room.

"D-Don't…"

Memories descend, sending a wave of bile up my throat. Pain. Agony, followed by a numb, weightless need to lie still and ignore the abuse happening to my body.

A rush of adrenaline counters the fear before it can consume me. *No!* Never will I endure that trauma again.

"Let go of me!" I lash out, nails drawn. Belatedly, I realize we've passed the billiard room, and I hold back, inches from gouging at his skin.

I blame my love for Franco solely for the restraint I find next. Bit by bit, I manage to reassemble my armor seconds before I'm pulled into another room. This one, is blissfully empty, decorated in shades of black and steel gray. It looks like an office, with a view of a darkened courtyard instead of the populated pool below.

"You want me? Then here you go, Lupe," Jaguar growls, releasing my arm. Even though he's seemingly capitulated to my request, a new fear takes root. Sex with several men is a chilling prospect, but intimacy with *one* man who doesn't care if he inflicts pain is a phobia I've yet to overcome.

Can I do so now on such short notice? My palms are sweating, my chest tight—but there is no choice. When Pedro's script becomes harder to grasp, I devise my own performance on the fly.

Eyeing Julian Domingas, I picture the one thing in the world I want most. Freedom. An escape from constant fear and anxiety and pain. In him, I pretend to see a future of sunshine and roses, and I let my hesitation fade away.

When he reaches for me, I relax into his grip, leaning against the nearest wall for stability. I make my expression playful and arch my back—but my facade cracks when his hands roughly grope my breasts. Gone is the pretty fantasy. I see a monster who takes what he wants.

In him, I see Diego Mendez.

"You're a convincing liar, Lupe," Jaguar murmurs against my neck when I stiffen. "But up close, I can sense your little act for what it is. Bullshit. You're shaking at my touch, beautiful. You don't seem very eager for me after all."

Inhaling deeply, I attempt to meet his gaze. "You're wrong," I lie. "It's anticipation. Not fear."

"Oh? You talk as though you have a magic pussy," he says, his breath hot on my throat. "Let's see if you can back it up."

Cutting to the chase, he plunges a hand beneath my skirt.

And I panic. *God no.* As his fingers brush my inner thigh, I feel a frantic sensation like pins and needles. This was a bad idea. Foolish.

But, he isn't Diego. I tell myself that over and over as he nudges the gusset of my panties with what feels like a thumb. With Julian Domingas, there is no expectation of forever. No complicated emotions. No heartrending betrayal.

This…

This is just business and believing that somehow makes it easier.

I spread my legs for him and force a moan through my damp lips before I remember another one of Pedro's warnings. *No faking, Pita. They can sense that. You give them real squirming, wincing, ouchie reactions? They'll eat it up like fucking candy.*

I don't have long to switch tact. He wrenches on the delicate elastic, pulling the fabric out of place, and slides a single finger inside me. "So tight," he grunts, sounding genuinely surprised.

Trying to register the intrusion, I close my eyes. He's right —it's a tight fit. To be fair, it's been so long since I've had anyone's fingers but my own up there. My first instinct is to suppress. Pretend. Gasp and wiggle my hips like a good girl and let him feel so damn masculine.

But I don't. I peel my eyes open instead and visibly wince. Maybe Pedro had it all wrong, but I find I'm incapable of doing anything else—reacting honestly.

Jaguar's eyebrow shoots up—in confusion rather than suspicion. "Am I hurting you?"

Roughly, he drags that finger in and out of me, widening my entrance and sowing searing friction. I can't silence a gasp. His hands are calloused and riddled with texture. The hardened skin snags on tender flesh, but the moisture that slicks his way in response comes as a shock to us both.

"No," I rasp, holding his probing stare.

"It seems you may be eager after all, Lupe," he grates, drawing back. The obvious sign of arousal glistening on his fingertips seems to lessen the coldness in his gaze. With that same hand, he reaches for the fastening of his pants.

I don't move to assist him. I just watch, oddly entranced by the organ that appears as he undoes his fly and lets the material fall down his hips.

For a second time, I am forced to use the word beautiful when describing him. He doesn't shave or keep himself trim the way some do. He's natural and wild, as if daring any woman to balk at the raw, primal energy he exudes.

When I don't, he makes a low sound in his throat. Approval? A jolt shoots through me, and I brace myself for the hungry way he grips my hips next, lifting me to him. I barely have a chance to hook my knee around his waist before he moves in, snatching my panties down my legs.

He doesn't play games or beat around the bush—literally. He slams himself home without giving a damn if I can take him or not.

And I can't. Until I am. He rips into me heedless of my body's natural response—but the tightening, clamping muscles seem to thrill him. He groans again.

I savor it as a sign that I've done something right—finally—but another concern gnaws away at me before I can help it. Ten years ago, I'd accustomed myself to the brutality of sex. Making love, we used to call it. He would shove me down, climb on top of me without preamble, and I truly believed that was what love felt like. A man invading my body, utilizing it as a warm wet hole without a single damn given for my soul.

That idiot teenager grew up into a woman who learned that intimacy wasn't supposed to hurt or be endured.

With that knowledge comes a set of impulses I can't suppress, not even now.

"S-Stop!" I grip his shoulder, but to my surprise, he goes still.

"Is this the game you're playing at?" he growls, fisting a hand through my hair, destroying my bun. "Talk a big game but wind up biting off more than you can chew." His eyes shoot to a color akin to midnight, and I know I'm treading on dangerous ground.

But he still obeyed my request, and my mind reels at that.

I can feel his cock pulsating against my inner thigh. It seems insane that he could be aroused this fast, and yet he still maintains a semblance of control. It's a surprisingly good sign.

"No." I meet his glare and hold it. Then I use my grip on his shoulder to adjust my hips, widening my legs a bit more.

He lunges, bucking into me without preamble, but I hiss through clenched teeth.

"Slow," I choke out. "Go slow. Please—" I add as he scoffs, and his expression betrays that waning interest again.

Thinking fast, I arch my back, taking his girth with another visible wince, but this way, I can feel the actual shape of his cock rather than forceful pressure. He feels strange inside me. So large but wickedly thick. With every twitching thrust, I can sense individual veins snaking up and down the considerable length.

Placated by the motion, Jaguar rocks into me, but noticeably slower.

A sound rips from my throat I can't name. He's too much. My eyelids lower as I rest my head against the wall.

He thrusts again. Again. Harder. Deeper, but with a persistent pulsing rhythm that is unlike anything I've ever felt. The man moves like an ocean wave. Unyielding. Unending. Unrestrained, he has the approach of a sledgehammer. But this way...

He's delicious fullness and devastating movement. I don't have to fake the pleasure—it comes on its own in illogical snatches. When his nails bite into my hips again. When he grates his pleasure against my ear. This must be a new sensation for him because he seems to relish it. How slow and controlled he can move. The variety of groans he can wrench from me.

In retrospect, I thought enduring him would be the hard part—but it's this. Knowing that my body can derive some twisted sense of satisfaction from impersonal fucking. I must be more tainted by Diego's violence than I realized.

How pathetic is that? Even a stranger can get me off as long as he allows me a fraction of control. Unashamed, I feed off every measured thrust, and a steady, persistent heat floods my body, making my toes curl with the force of it.

But then, he picks up the pace.

"You like it slow," he says into my ear. "But I like it *hard*, chica. Like this."

He combines both methods, and the result makes me gasp out loud.

It's too good.

Scary good.

It terrifies me to admit that I could get used to this—which is so damn sad. How little it takes to satisfy someone broken like me. Just communication. The illusion of control. The pretense of power.

A taste of equality.

My body trembles as a feeling so alien that it takes me a moment to name it hits me all at once. An orgasm.

My legs go numb, and I cling to him as all the air leaves my lungs. I eye the ceiling struggling to remember the reason I'm here. Not for Jaguar. Not even for sex.

I need to convince this man that I'm his. That only I have what he needs—at least in exchange for what, in essence, would be mere child's play for him.

But to cement that ticket, I need to do something. Say something. Pedro told me the exact words, but meeting Jaguar's gaze now, I can't think of them. So, I ad lib.

"This is better than if you shared me," I tell him. "It will always be better between us this way."

"Will it?" His expression falls, and those eyes close up, leaving me with a sensation akin to whiplash.

"Lupita with the magic pussy." He shoves me off him and wrestles himself back into his pants. "I think it's time for you to go, sweetheart." His sly grin returns with chilling intensity, and my heart stutters. I've done something wrong. "Thank you for the quickie."

An overwhelming sense of disappointment sweeps through me. My first impulse is to resist. Argue. Get angry.

Instead, I nod, smoothing my skirt into place. "Thank you. Is it too much trouble to ask for a ride? If not, I have a friend I could call."

Please, give me a ride. It's my one hope that all of this hasn't been a total waste. *Trust Pedro,* I chant, my internal mantra. *Follow his plan.*

Jaguar chuckles to himself. "It seems my driver is busy tonight. I guess you'll have to find your own way."

Don't show you're insulted.

Nodding again, I walk into the hall. With every step, I feel his seed run down my thigh. He didn't use a condom, though I have a birth control implant, at least. That doesn't calm the voice in my head warning me that I've been so stupid. Reckless.

Foolish.

When I reach the first floor, I call a car service and linger in the foyer under the watchful eye of a stern-faced doorman. A gaggle of giggling women, dripping wet, wearing string bikinis skip down the hall. They pass me knowing glances before heading upstairs, no doubt to wait on their master hand and foot.

Focus, Lupita.

When my car arrives, I leave, and thus is a rather anticlimactic ending to my night.

But my mental turmoil is just beginning.

Stupid! Stupid!

The second I'm out of view of the mansion, I call Pedro, fighting back tears.

"Pita?" He sounds tired, his voice hushed. "You're still alive, at least. That must account for something."

"It didn't work." Only now does it sink in how much I've gambled away on a silly plan—and badly lost. "God, it didn't work. What am I going to do? I wasted too much time. That bastard will be at the airport and—"

"I'll tell you what you're going to do—go to the address we talked about, and you wait there for at least a day. Trust me, if you did what I told you to, you have him hooked. He'll call on you. If not, I won't have you fuck up everything by linking yourself back to me. Go to the address and stay the night."

"But—"

"No buts. Do it. Yes?" His voice is muffled as if he moved his mouth from the phone. "Coming, Papi."

"Wait! Pedro?" The line goes dead, and I slump into my seat, hopeless.

The address he gave me leads to an upscale apartment building downtown. *It's important you go there after,* he told me during the hasty prep for this insane plan. *It's neutral territory. If he decides to track you down, he won't be able to trace anything from there. If you fuck up and go to my apartment or yours, the jig is up, Pita. This is the most vital part of the plan.*

Wait while Franco gets on a plane and takes off for God knows where.

I've trusted Pedro up until this point, but in this instance…

"I need to make a detour," I tell the driver.

He inclines his head with a shrug. "Where to?"

Somewhere I promised myself I would never set foot near again.

CHAPTER FIVE

Braulio has an array of mansions to hide in, and my prior attempts to pin him down have resulted in nothing but frustration and heartache. But now…

Maybe it's fate—a cruel joke on God's part to reinforce just how much he's forsaken me. I pick a house at random, but this time the lights are on, illuminating the entire dwelling and the hillside it resides upon. I can't get close enough to it to make out anyone of substance—Braulio doesn't share Jaguar's blatant confidence in his safety. He's as fearful as a mouse in a trap, and he should be.

Even though I can't see him, I can feel Francisco nearby. God, I hope he can feel me and knows I will never let him go—not without a fight.

The itching drive to scale the outer wall of the complex and break inside rises up in me so fiercely it takes all of my restraint to quash it. In a trembling voice, I tell the driver to move on, and we arrive back at Pedro's apartment just after midnight.

It's a nice place. Too nice for his tastes, and I can tell he doesn't spend much time here if he even owns it directly. In any case, it's a fitting backdrop for the woman I've pretended to be. A pristine, lifeless façade who gives her body to the first man who offers her a way out.

Exhausted, I shower in a beautiful walk-in large enough for four people, but the walls still feel as though they're closing in. Once I exit, wrapped in a towel, I don't sleep in the large bed.

I pace, raking my fingers through my wet hair as Pedro's dress dries in the bathroom.

I try calling him again, but he doesn't answer.

By the time dawn rolls around, I have to face the truth alone without my friend's comfort. I failed. Whatever I did wasn't enough to grab Jaguar's interest. I'll have to start from ground zero and track Francisco the hard way. First, I'll find where Braulio is and demand he tell me his whereabouts himself.

Maybe you'll sleep with him too, a cruel part of me whispers. *You seem to like spreading it around after all this time.*

The realization stings. Diego was the last man to ever touch me, and for the life of me… I can't even remember what it felt like. I can recall the pain, yes—to the degree that it feels as fresh and raw as the day he first slammed his fist into my skull for "back talk." But not what he felt like. Not if I'd truly felt any pleasure. I can't remember if I ever came with him inside me, moaning like a whore.

I can't remember when it ever felt good.

I can't remember ever craving him internally. Not wanting but craving. Like an itch has taken root inside my skin, but one I can't ever reach. Only blunt force can. Pressure and unrelenting touch.

I hate that I can't get that monster out of my head. At least I'll end this debacle with a souvenir—I finally have an even bigger mistake to forget than Diego. This time, however, I had a lucky escape.

But avoiding Jaguar seems to be where my good fortune has run out. By the time daylight pierces the horizon, I know it's over. Braulio is out of the country, and I've failed Franco yet again.

Despite him avoiding my calls, I owe Pedro enough that I wait until the end of his deadline. Noon. Or, at least, I wait until eleven. Just as I head for the door, my phone rings, and I retreat into the bathroom, if only so no one in the hallway can hear me screaming.

"About time you answer me, Pedro. You twisted bastard—"

"I did what you asked me to do. I didn't guarantee any returns. Besides, you got a nice night outside of your shitty apartment out of it. And more. My little Pita placing big bets. I didn't expect you to win it back for me," he says, sounding smug.

"Win what?" I ask, only to remember the cage fight.

"You won big last night, honey. I took out my cut, but the rest is already in your account. Over a hundred grand, baby. Now say 'thank you, Pedro.'"

"Fuck you, Pedro." I slump against the counter and watch my expression turn to despair over the mirror's surface. It's more money than I could dream of owning and I'm too devastated to care. "What am I going to do? I… I can't lose him. I can't."

"I know," Pedro says softly. "I probably shouldn't tell you this, but I know for a fact that Braulio's private plane left from a remote airport last night. He's gone, Pita. You know I'll do whatever I can, but for now, I want you to take a break. There's nothing else you can do about it, so breathe. Enjoy the place for another day. Try out the jacuzzi bathtub. I'll call you when I'm done with my next appointment. Ciao, bella."

He hangs up, and I don't know how much time passes before I finally gather the nerve to head into the hall. I'm wearing the dress from last night, still, damp after my attempt at handwashing it in the sink. Apparently, I didn't do a good enough job because I can still smell him all over me. Jaguar. God, his scent is poisonous, infecting every pore. The air itself…

In fact, it's too real, and I think I know even before I round the corner what I'll find, there in the living room. A Jaguar in the flesh.

He's leaning against the kitchen counter, that smirk playing across his lips. Today he's opted for a black, button-up shirt with the buttons mostly undone, revealing more tattoos that span his chest. With difficulty, I resist examining them fully and instead turn my focus to his face and those probing, fathomless eyes.

"Little Lupe," he greets in a guttural tone. "If you know me as well as you claim, you would know better than to lie to me."

My blood runs cold. Apparently, he isn't here to reassure my fears that I've lost his interest—this isn't a friendly visit. "About what?" I ask when I find my nerve again.

He laughs, but there's no mirth in it. "Well, for starters… You can't be Lupita Sanchez, because she is dead."

Oh. It's funny how you can forget so many trivial things while living off the grid. Birthdays of old acquaintances. Holidays. Tax laws.

The fact that you've been legally dead for ten years.

I'm too shocked to recover, and he cocks his head in triumph.

"You really didn't think I'd look into your little story? After all, you dared me to." He advances a step, and I can't help it.

I jump back, and my gaze darts to the only exit.

"Don't play the shy role now," he scolds, clucking his tongue. Just like that, he's paces closer, eating up the space between us with calculated, predatory strides. "You were so eager to please me last night—"

"And then you turned me down, if I recall," I counter, raising my chin. The venom in my tone seems to surprise us both. He raises an eyebrow and, internally, I'm berating myself. Do I really want to piss off the unofficial king of this entire region?

Maybe. Especially if he stands between Franco and me. I've already wasted too much ground playing this stupid game. It will take days to track where the plane went. Even longer to find Braulio's latest hideout.

I don't have time for delays, not even when presented by a psychotic narco with a power complex.

"You turned me down, Jaguar," I point out coldly. "Braulio is gone, and our deal is forfeit. You got a 'quickie' out of it, though. Unfortunately, I don't think we have anything left to discuss."

"Oh, but we do." He gestures toward a leather couch positioned near a view of the city. "Have a seat."

I don't move. My heart is pounding, my palms slick with sweat. All in all, this should be a familiar feeling—déjà vu. It's been a long time since I've been around Diego, but I remember what it was like. A bit like living with a hissing viper poised to strike. There was a reason why he called me his butterfly—I had to be agile always.

Facing Jaguar inspires a different kind of thrill, but I know the fun and games won't last long. Sooner or later, he'll turn on me, and I suspect feline fangs hurt far worse than a snake's.

"I know for a fact that Braulio is gone," I reiterate, crossing my arms to disguise how my hands shake. "With him, went my only bargaining chip. Frankly, I think we're both wasting our time."

"Are we?" He claims the couch for himself, his legs spread wide, hands on his knees. "You certainly didn't find it a waste of time to fuck me instead of tailing Braulio yourself. Don't pretend this is about a fucking plane."

"You're right," I snap. "It's about Franc—my son."

"That's another thing." He holds up a finger as if to keep track of my supposed lies. "According to all public records, Lupita Sanchez never had a son. There is another woman by the name of Sanchez who does, however. A son named Francisco Roberto Rivera. That woman is not named Lupe —though I honestly prefer it. In any case, it's nice to make your acquaintance, Tiena. I will admit, I prefer you as a brunette than a blond."

I don't know what to do. What to say. Technically, he's right. I fit all the plausible criteria to be only one woman— barring the fact that she's far more likely to be dead than I am. Still, using her identity puts one more layer between Jaguar and me. Suddenly space from him seems like a very smart course of action to take—besides, coming clean now could provoke him further.

So, I decide to thread the needle as carefully as I can.

"You know the risk I was taking by meeting you alone," I say. It isn't quite a lie.

"And you know that I prefer honesty." His upper lip quirks. Is he shocked by how easily I cop to the ruse? He shouldn't be. At least someone is fighting for Franco. In a twisted irony, I am his mother, if not in name, then in spirit.

"You have some balls promising that you'll belong to me alone. I'm sure you also realize that I know you've been around far more men than you've led on," he says, but there's an odd dip in his inflection. What he's saying should be true, but for some reason, he doesn't believe it. "Braulio was just the latest in your string of rich, powerful men, chica."

I could deny it, but something I can't name won't let me. "You felt me for yourself. Did I feel like a woman who's had a stream of men before you?"

He frowns, but I recognize that anger isn't the source. He can hear the truth in my voice, and it doesn't quite square with the woman I should be. Does it please some small part of me to have fooled him? Yes, but I'm not brazen enough to believe it will last. Sooner or later, he'll turn the tables, and I can't let this round of our game get that far.

"You had a tight pussy, I'll give you that," he says in a voice devoid of emotion. "But I don't tolerate being lied to. You should be punished."

I've heard those words before—several variations of them, in fact. *I'll hurt you. You'll be sorry for that. I will kill you, Lupita. Do you hear me? Kill you.*

But his voice… It didn't contain the malice I'm used to hearing. I feel my belly flip, but not in a way that signals terror. As my gaze settles on those thick hands, a fleeting thought crosses my mind—how would it feel to have those digits inside me while he murmurs that phrase into my ear? *Punished.*

I shake my head to clear it, and my heart is racing ten times faster. Jaguar is no longer my sole focus. Only Francisco.

"If you learned who I am, then you know how desperately I needed you to stop that plane."

"You mean this plane?" He reaches into the breast pocket of his shirt and withdraws a crisp stack of small squares which he lays out on the coffee table. Photographs. In one, I recognize a familiar, precious face, and I lunge for it.

"Franco…" He looks so sad. So tired, but clean, at least. There are no fresh bruises from what I can tell. Not like that day just a couple months ago when he came home from school, and Tiena had the nerve to feign that nothing was wrong.

It's just a mark, Pita. Why do you have your panties all in a bunch?

A mark. She actually said that despite acknowledging the hell we both grew up in. Bruises like that are never accidental.

Even in the dim lighting, I can tell that one on Franco's face has yet to truly fade. God only knows what Braulio's been doing to him since he cut me off—though this photo was taken at night, obscuring most of his body. The area around him looks like… A tarmac?

The series of pictures beside it paints a clearer view. Braulio did send Franco on a plane, but Jaguar had someone there for takeoff and the landing, it seems. They didn't go as far as I feared. California. He's still in the country.

And Jaguar's photographer apparently took a snapshot of the exact safe house he's being kept in.

One figure's glaring disappearance, however, stands out.

"I don't see Braulio." I look up to find Jaguar watching me, his expression unreadable.

"That's because he's still in the city," he finally says. I get the sense he was gauging my reaction carefully. Another test. Did I pass? I can't tell. "It seems he had an urgent matter come up overnight that required his attention. He'll be busy for a few days, at least."

But, for the time being, Franco is safe in another state, far away from him. Yet, I get the sense this change of fate isn't by coincidence. The truth bites into me slowly, and I feel my eyes widen.

"You upheld our bargain," I croak.

"I always pay my debts," he replies, folding his hands over his lap. "But being lied to? That was not a part of our deal. You offered me your soul, after all."

"I offered you *me*," I say. "You weren't interested."

He sits forward, and my breath catches. I have that quicksand feeling again. One wrong move, and I'll go under.

"Now, when did I say that?" He looks me over, as if noting for the first time that I'm still wearing the dress from last night. My hair is a mess, my makeup gone, and eyes bloodshot. My saving grace, I suppose, is that I don't look like a woman who plays the game. The real Tiena would be in another man's bed by now, safely secured with whatever she desired. She was resourceful like that, more than I ever was.

"I prefer to do business over dinner," he says finally, leaning back into the couch. "Be ready at seven. Make yourself presentable. If you even think about showing up late or playing the tricks your kind like to play, you will regret it." He stands and heads for the door. In the next moment, he stops, his head inclined, his face turned away from me. "Oh, and one more thing… You were on the phone with someone when I came in. Who?"

Despite my naiveté, I recognize another test that goes beyond simple word games. Those were petty fun. This is life or death—a primed trap with metal teeth waiting to snap shut over a tender limb.

My first instinct is to lie. At the last moment, I rethink it. Pedro is the most important person in the world to me besides Franco. I won't betray him.

But I promised Jaguar my loyalty.

"A friend," I say carefully. "Someone who is no threat to you. He's helped me get what I needed but nothing else."

"What you needed…" He laughs. It's a low, unsettling dance of sound, but though I strain my ears… I don't find disappointment or anger lurking within it. Perhaps surprise?

I told him as much of the truth as possible without revealing all the cards I have at my disposal.

My gut tells me he would have done the same thing if he were in my place.

What a dangerous way to think.

CHAPTER SIX

When he leaves, I don't know what to do. Mainly because I'm not sure he's really gone. A prickling sensation on the back of my neck won't go away. Pedro's apartment seems as safe as ever, but I feel eyes on me. Would I put it past a man like Jaguar to have cameras secretly installed in the home of a potential ally?

Hell no, I wouldn't.

Yet, I can't deny that this paranoia differs from what I remember enduring with Diego. There is no suffocating fear that I'm breathing incorrectly. Moving wrong. Blinking wrong.

In this case, there is only a persistent awareness. I have Julian Domingas' attention—and I dare not disappoint him.

The first thing I do when I regain my senses is call Pedro. My panicked voice must convince him to put aside his latest paramour for five minutes. When I finish telling him what happened, he curses in a string of Spanish and whistles through his teeth.

"Damn. It actually worked. Holy shit. You hooked Julian fucking Domingas. What the hell were you thinking?"

"I haven't hooked anyone," I snap, leaning against the bathroom mirror. The blurry reflection of myself stares at me skeptically. *You're a damn liar,* her eyes say. I turn my back to her. "I caught his interest," I tell Pedro, "but trust me, he'll tire of me by tomorrow. The point is, he got Braulio away from Franco. I know where he is. I'll text you a picture of the house. If you could help me use one of your contacts—"

"Oh no, *puta*," he snaps. "No way in hell am I getting involved any more than I already have. You're in with the cartel now, Pita. If I had any damn sense, I would hang up on your stupid ass."

"But you haven't," I say, switching to the whining tone I know he can't resist. "Pedro, I can't do this. Not without your help. Please don't abandon me now. Remember when I kicked that coyote bastard who called you the f-word when we came over? He hit me so hard I couldn't taste anything for a week."

That was just one harrowing part of a hellish three-week ordeal that landed us in this backwater part of Texas. Still, it was better than the nightmare we escaped from.

"Pita…" I hear a muffled bit of movement come from the other end. Then a sigh. "You're a bitch to bring that up. Besides, he only yelled at me because we kept falling behind because of that fucking backpack filled with books you made us carry. Still, there is one silver lining to your situation. Jaguar *will* tire of you eventually. Play your cards right, and you'll last a week at most and can retire with your own fancy crash pad and perhaps a new car. Hell, he could give you far more than that, but trust me. He won't want more than a few days at most."

"Your confidence in me is inspiring, Pedro."

"You need more than confidence," he says. "Besides, you should pray that I'm right. Men like Jaguar love sex, but don't do commitment."

"I know," I admit. "In any case, I need an outfit for tonight. All I have on me is your dress."

"Well, that I can help with. I have a girl I go to. I'll hook you up. Jaguar will be well entertained while you do have his attention, at least." After he falls silent, a bit of doubt creeps in.

"I… I'm scared, Pedro," I admit, hating the tremor in my voice. "How far do I even take this?"

"As far as you need to," he says in an abnormally serious tone. "You're doing this for Franco, Pita. Think about him, and you'll survive. You don't have a choice."

He's right, my old friend. In more ways than one.

"I guess this means I'll need to commandeer your place for a few more days."

"After the motherlode you won the other night? Consider it yours. I'll even have it put in your name—"

"No, not my name," I rasp. "Pedro, he thinks… He thinks I'm Tiena."

"*Dios mío!*" He whistles again, with far more exasperation. "How the hell did you step into that mess?"

"I don't know. Maybe because we're identical twins?"

"Identical, minus her resting bitch-face, fake tits, bleached as fuck hair, and split ends."

I ignore Pedro's commentary. "*Also…* Because on paper Lupita Sanchez is legally dead?"

The phrase sounds so frightening when spoken aloud. So finite. To be fair, I've mostly stayed off the radar out of an abundance of caution, rather than anything else. Diego has been dead for a long, long time. In his absence, I simply forgot to resurrect myself.

"You're right," Pedro says, drawing me back to the present. "It's been so damn long I forgot about that."

"And you're the one who got me my bank accounts and passport," I point out. Each time I use them, I have to refresh my memory of the name, Maria something. Luckily, I rarely leave the city and get paid under the table at my bartending job.

"I'll make arrangements and see if I can get a hold of Tiena's shit," Pedro suggests. "If the rumors are true, she won't be needing it."

"Cold, Pedro," I scold without real anger in my voice. "She's still my sister, dead or alive."

"Yeah, and that's your burden to bear. She's the same sister who left you behind in Tijuana and made you do her dirty work just to stay under her roof. Don't forget that she made you run shit for Braulio once upon a time."

"I remember," I say thickly. How could I forget the condition my sister placed on letting me stay with her, under the radar?

"As far as I'm concerned, she's just a stranger with your face," Pedro goes on. "Your evil twin, so to speak. You've been dancing around the issue, but *she's* the real reason you've been forced to go to someone like Jaguar. You're fighting harder for her damn child than she ever did. I didn't help you for *her*, by the way. I did it for you. I'm sure the sex was incredible. It's about time you lived a little."

I should deny it, I think. Instead, I sigh.

"I have to go, Pedro, but if I call you again, the least you can do is answer the damn phone."

"*Sí, mami.* Also, I shouldn't have to tell you this, but if you start going around town claiming to be Tiena, word will get back to you know who. Braulio has ears everywhere. You'll need protection. Make sure you whisper a desire for a bodyguard in Jaguar's ear. I'll do what I can on my end to give you a heads-up should I hear anything on the grapevine."

He hangs up, but his advice lingers ominously in the air. As per usual, he has a damn point, and he's far more used to this lifestyle than I am. Still, I decide to worry about Braulio later.

After splashing water on my face, I glance at my phone and discover a message from Pedro with an address for a boutique. I take another car service there, and roughly three hours later, I return to the apartment armed with a new dress and at least a week's worth of designer clothing.

Pedro sure did make sure to cover all the bases. There is lingerie and several underwear sets, all more expensive than my go-to cotton pairs back in my own place. I briefly consider heading there for my own things, but decide against it.

All day, I've felt watched. I swear I saw the same car going to and coming from the boutique. Jaguar's had me followed, alright. Either that or Braulio has already gotten wind of his ex-lover back from exile.

The funny part is if Tiena were to reappear, she'd pull a stunt like this. Ingratiate herself with a more powerful figure and use him to exact revenge. Then she'd probably get pregnant again and leave that child the second something better came along.

At least in that small way, I differ from her. Diego most likely ruined my chances of ever having children, though I will still take every precaution when it comes to Jaguar.

Such as heeding his deadlines.

I shower again and arrange my damp hair into a simple low bun. I select a modest red dress, eerily similar to the black one I wore last night. It might be a matter of playing it safe, or I just like the symbolism behind it. While today may be a different day, I am still involved in a dangerous dance of fate.

And I still have to earn his attention—enough to convince him to ruin Braulio for good. Or perhaps get Franco away from him. We would go into hiding together then. Pedro would have no problem procuring new documents for us both and…

What? a part of me scoffs. A happily fucking ever after? I'd outgrown fairy tale stories years ago, when life with Diego taught me the hard, bitter truth one can't find in romance novels. In reality, love is pain. It's a name we assign to broken, jagged emotions and the masking tape we use to obscure how bleak our lives truly are. It took me years to realize that Diego never loved me.

He merely owned me and nearly broke me.

What does Jaguar plan to do when he eventually grows bored of my presence? I can only hope he casts me aside like a gently used toy and moves on. I'd be fine with that. Then I could take Franco and finally live a better life than the one I left behind.

But that would require pleasing him in the meantime—a task I find increasingly difficult given that he never gave me a number to call or even a location to wait for him. By seven-oh-one, I risk leaving the apartment and head down to the lobby.

There, I find no one. I'm ready to write it off as a cruel exercise in being stood up when my cell phone buzzes. Only Pedro has this number, so I ignore it in favor of panicking. I even go outside, but there isn't a car waiting. Neither do I find Jaguar scowling down at his watch.

Pedro texts me again. Then again, in quick succession. That isn't like him. Annoyed, I fish my phone from my pocket and open the first message.

You're late.

The number isn't from Pedro's main cell or his two known burners. In fact, I don't recognize it, but the tone of the message does trigger a sense of familiarity.

Jaguar.

You should know what kind of man I am, Lupe, he added. *You don't want to waste my time.*

I whirl around, scanning the empty lobby. Then it hits me —he's already here.

I race up to the fifth floor and tentatively open the door to my borrowed apartment. Seated on the couch, cell phone in hand, is Jaguar, appearing as though he never left. He's even wearing the same dark ensemble.

"I didn't know you'd come to me," I rasp as those piercing eyes flick in my direction. He's angry. The air prickles with the telltale stench of his displeasure, and I shiver. "You're a busy man," I add in a halfhearted attempt to plead my case.

But it's too late.

"And you seem to be a busy woman."

I'm sweating, my breath escaping in pants. Like I ran here —which I did—but I suspect that's not the conclusion he's come to. I look like I've been with someone else, only to come crawling to him once finished.

And it's a suspicion I know in my gut I need to dispel ASAP.

Entering the apartment, I close the door with my hip and approach him, moving slowly so that he can see I only have my purse. It's the way Braulio likes to be approached, though Diego preferred a different tactic.

To avoid a beating, I had to be all but on my hands and knees.

"I thought I would come to you," I tell Jaguar. "My apartment is nowhere near worthy of hosting you for dinner—"

"*Your* apartment," he parrots in an unnervingly deep tone. First test, failed. "Your apartment where you keep no clothes. No photographs. Nothing personal whatsoever. You think I don't recognize a stash house when I see one?"

He has a point, and only God knows what Pedro really uses this place for. I could lie, of course. Spin a good tale.

But I promised this man my honesty, and he'll get it. A distilled, carefully-sanitized version of it.

"It took you less than a day to figure out who I really am," I tell him, inching closer though my heart lurches at his cold expression. It's normal to feel fear, but... This feeling is more akin to when he dragged me into that office and pressed me against the wall. Terrifying and thrilling. "How much easier would it be for Braulio?"

"And that is why you have nothing in your name?" he murmurs, stroking his chin with a dangerous flick of his thumb. "Even your number was hard to find, chica. You cost a pretty penny to track down, and none of the men seemingly footing the bill for your accounts have ever been publicly photographed with you. And you, Tiena. You have been photographed with many, *many* men."

"And you have a harem of women on your arm," I point out, but my tone is playful. God, I hope he interprets it as playful.

When I come close enough, he extends a hand in my direction. His grip isn't bruising but firm enough that I can't easily pull away as he maneuvers me to sit on his thigh.

"I was with only one man last night," I say, hating the hitch in my voice. It sounds too damn genuine. Too...excited?

"So you say." His hand settles over my thigh with a familiarity that has me quaking. Boldly, without preamble, he slides those searching fingers beneath my skirt...beneath my panties...inside me.

My head rears back, caught against his shoulder. It should hurt, I think. Feel debasing. Rough. Wrong. Instead, his touch feels…

Like fire, igniting a part of me I never knew could be this sensitive.

"You have been busy," he says, his voice thick with disapproval. Deliberately, his finger prods deeper, and whatever he feels makes him laugh in a chilling way. "Either that or you are just *very* happy to see me, Tiena."

I choke at the realization of what has him so skeptical—my passage is already slick with arousal. I'm not used to this feeling. This damp ache that eases his movements inside of me. That's why it doesn't hurt. Rather than tense in discomfort at the intrusion, I can relish the thick shape— but it's nowhere thick enough to rival the fullness from last night.

There isn't time to marvel at the sensation. He's furious, and I only have seconds to think of a way to calm him. In this instance, the truth alone should do the trick.

"I told you it would be different between us," I rasp—but that husky murmur doesn't sound like me. The real Tiena, perhaps, when she's working on her latest mark. When she tells her lover the dirty things she'll do for him and let him do to her. She never means it, but in this case…

"Ah," he agrees, his tone still caustic. "Because now I have a magic dick in addition to your magic pussy."

"You felt it," I manage to croak out. As if to punish me, he adds a second finger beside the first, and I can't help but shift my hips to adjust. With my legs spread wider, he can reach even deeper, and I long for that pulsing friction.

"Felt what? Your pussy? I hate to fracture your pride, but it didn't feel like magic to me, chica."

I bat the insult aside, sensing what he doesn't say. Last night wasn't magic, perhaps, but it was different than what he expected. Different from what he is used to.

"I've never had sex like that," I confess, panting heavily. He can hear my honesty, but rather than reassure him, that angry stench grows stronger. His touch becomes firmer, more assured. It's like he's searching for any trace of another, daring me to admit it.

I'm lying.

"And you've had plenty of sex, it seems," he murmurs against my throat, but his tone is softer by a fraction, though no less unsettling. "Not many women would let a stranger ride them bareback. Even those in my so-called harem blanche at doing so the first time."

"It felt good," I hear myself blurt. Who the hell is that whore of a woman? Someone unashamed by her need for him. This act has gone too far already. I'm starting to scare myself.

Hopefully, my supposed eagerness will only accelerate my eventual goal of letting him bore of me before it gets too late. Men hate women who seem to fall too fast. They love a challenge. Risk. My fake version of Tiena doesn't present one. She's too damn easy, writhing on his lap from his touch alone.

But faking is one thing. Genuine pleasure is another matter entirely, and I am not able to conceal it. As it drips from me, he relishes the aftermath, teasing the dampening flesh at his mercy. When he switches from the calloused tip of the finger to what can only be a nail, the pinching graze is sinful.

I choke, squirming on his knee.

"You're saying I felt good?" Jaguar's mouth is at my ear again, and another sharp pain alludes to what he does next —bite my earlobe hard enough to make me jump. "Are you sure about that? I will admit you put on a different show than most. No screaming. No moans. No praises that I'm too big."

And he is, but I'm horrified to admit I didn't mind it. Not when he let me set the pace.

"You fail when it comes to faking it, Lupe," he concludes in disapproval. "I didn't feel magic when I came inside of you. I felt a woman who has never felt a real fucking in her goddamn life."

He isn't wrong. *Dios mío,* he isn't.

But then why is he still angry? Furious, even. I can taste his rage, and it alone should leave me in a quivering heap, cringing for his first blow. Instead, I arch my back and focus again on how strangely satisfying he feels.

I need to convince him to maintain my ruse, but I feel as though I'm on the precipice of a more dangerous venture. There is a risk of going too far, of saying too much.

Then he thrusts those fingers hard and fast, and I lose all sense of logical reasoning. "Speak," he grates.

"You weren't what I expected," I tell him, gasping for air. "Not what I wanted—"

"Oh?" He laughs a second time, and I don't know whether it's fear I feel shooting through me or something far worse. "Did my magic dick not please little Lupe after all?"

He wants me to say yes. It seems he feeds on the prospect of rejection. Not because he loves a good chase, but because it would support his conclusions about me.

That I'm an enemy, someone he can't trust.

It's harder than it should be to angle my head to meet his stare. The smirk on his face has never been wider than it is now. The second our gazes meet, it falls, however. A strange tension comes over him next, hardening the line of his mouth.

Once again, I'm in dangerous territory, and for the life of me, I can't decide which action to take. Pedro didn't foresee this encounter, and I have no script to fall back on.

So, I tell him the truth.

"I've dealt with countless men like you," I confess—though most of those men could be found in just one, Diego. He could be both lover, teacher. Tormentor, too. Judge, jury, and executioner. All in one. Then there is Braulio and those in his vicinity. So yes, technically, it isn't a lie. "None of them ever made me feel…"

Raw. He slides his fingers out of me and jams them back in. The sensation makes my head reel. I lose my train of thought, and I don't have the sense of mind to make my words pretty to flatter him.

"You gave me a taste of power," I blurt out. "I want more."

"More." He chuckles. Whatever I said wasn't exactly what he expected—it's better. I've pleased him though he won't admit it. He shows it by stroking me a fraction softer. Then he pairs the gentleness with force by spreading those two fingers apart, stretching me around him. "Telling me that you like it slow? I'm sure you moan that line to all your lovers."

And maybe I have in the past, but none of those pleas were ever heeded. I don't tell him that, though. I let him put the pieces together on his own. Even hearing him throw those words back in my face does something to me. My body feels hotter. The pressure inside me grows. I feel like a tire with too much air inside, one wrong move from bursting altogether.

"I told you that if you wanted me, you would have me," I croak. "All of me."

And apparently, it wasn't good enough for him. I could live with that. I can't fathom the effect he seems to have on me without even trying.

I'm seconds away from coming undone, and he's only used his damn fingers. After surviving Diego, I learned to trust my one remaining shred of self-preservation, and it is telling me to run far and fast away from this man.

"But you're right," I say, bracing my hands against the massive body beneath me. Working myself off him is like surfacing after minutes spent underwater, a hairsbreadth from drowning. "You have access to plenty of women, all better trained than I am."

"Oh, I wouldn't say that, Lupe. My harem women are never this wet."

I blush as his fingers slide out of me. The sudden emptiness rocks me, but the clarity that floods my brain in response is a good sign. On trembling legs, I lurch upright. The window is my nearest anchor, and I stagger to it, bracing my hands against the glass. Without facing him, it's easier to maintain my ruse, though this time, the script isn't just meaningless words. Deep down, it's what I know to be the safest way out of this mess.

"I've bored you, Jaguar," I confess in between pants. "We can end this now. You showed me where Franco is. I can take it from here, and I will forever be grateful to you—"

"Come here."

I shudder at that authoritative tone, but I recognize there's no power behind it. He's testing me yet again, jerking me around like a puppet on a string.

And I obey. The gleam I find in his eyes tells me that he knows I had a choice, and I chose right. I've pleased him again—but he doesn't seem too thrilled about it.

When I reach him, he snags both of my wrists, forcing my arms out while my body is examined at his leisure by those roving eyes.

"You don't look like a pro," he says, observing my quivering legs. Is it meant to be an insult? Perhaps. Nevertheless, he seems appreciative of what he sees. His tongue traces his lower lip, an eyebrow raised. "Real ass. Real tits. Average-sized waist."

"I wouldn't insult you by giving you something inauthentic," I counter, suddenly self-conscious.

"The shit you say." He smirks, but it's one of the dangerous ones. My heart skips a beat. Then several more.

"That's been taught," he surmises with a knowing tilt of his head. "You've been trained well, chica, but I know a windup when I hear it."

He isn't exactly wrong, but the truth isn't anywhere close to what he thinks. Some sick part of me savors that—loves having one small bit of knowledge he doesn't. But a battle of wits with Julian Domingas is a perilous game.

"I'll let your mind games slide if you tell me the truth. What is it you really want?"

He already knows the real answer—Franco safe, a life far from Braulio. He's angling for something different, a more elusive want that amounts to fantasy more than anything else.

"I want to give myself to someone with no fear," I tell him. "I want protection. I never want to know pain again."

I feel like a child professing a desire to be a ballerina or an astronaut. Craving something far out of reach but near enough to touch.

He accepts that confession in silence, but I can't tell from his expression what he thinks of it.

"You think you know anything of fear?" His tone does that thing to me. My heart pangs, and I feel lightheaded. Weightless. "A woman, tossed around from narco to narco. It seems you've been sheltered from reality, Tiena."

"It seems," I parrot as he releases my arms in favor of palming my waist. "But appearances can be deceiving, Jaguar."

"That I know, chica." He releases me and stands, heading for the door. "Are you coming?" he asks when I don't follow.

Belatedly I remember our supposed date, but I feel that this entire buildup was yet another test. Mercifully I passed it, but at what cost? Something unspoken transpired between us, but I'm unsure exactly what it entailed. A promise, I think.

I claim to know fear. He aims to show me exactly how little I do.

And this is one bet I won't win.

CHAPTER SEVEN

He came via a different car from the SUV. It's an intimate sports car that he apparently drove himself, but I'm not fooled. A suspicious number of vehicles follow us out of the parking garage. Even so, I sense it's rare for him to be without his entourage. I'm curious enough to ask him about it.

"We won't be joined by your harem tonight?"

The back seat certainly isn't big enough for them all.

"Jealousy isn't an attractive trait, Tiena," he warns. He eyes the road, his head partially tilted in my direction. A coldness comes over him when he's deep in thought. It dampens his usual intensity, making him seem more distant —like a blazing inferno trapped in ice. "You know what is attractive? A woman who shuts her mouth and listens. I'm sure you listened to plenty of conversations Braulio might have had behind the scenes. Tell me about them."

Ah. It's a line of questioning I didn't anticipate, but I should have. A woman privy to the secrets of one powerful kingpin should be expected to gladly share those secrets with another. In theory.

"Discretion is attractive," I say demurely.

His head whips around to shoot me a probing glance. *Wrong answer.*

"You writhe on my lap and fuck yourself on my fingers. Then you play coy with providing the one thing of value a woman like you has. Some might find the act tiring."

I toy with the hem of my dress while processing his words. Tiring or stupid? His assessment should inspire fear, but it doesn't. Maybe I've become numb to common sense?

"And a man such as yourself would never respect a woman who rushes to spill her ex-lover's secrets," I reply. "My bargain was for myself alone. I'm sure you already know everything there is to know about Braulio and his business. Anything I tell you would be petty gossip, far beyond your business interests."

"You have a pretty little reply for everything, don't you? Tell me something else, and this time don't give me your rehearsed bullshit. I want an authentic answer, *sí?*"

I consider the request. It sounds harmless enough, but nothing ever is with him.

"Okay."

"What were you thinking of when you were fucking me? You were awfully soaked. Even my best girls don't gush like that."

My cheeks flame, and an impulsive reply rips out of me. "I don't know what you're talking about—"

He releases the wheel to capture my wrist with one hand. "No, don't give me that." The tone of his voice dips in a terrifying way. "I mean it. I've humored you until now, but I'm warning you. I'm growing tired of your game. Answer the question."

I squirm and fidget with my skirt, trapped into saying something. "I thought about... How different it felt to what I expected."

"Are you telling me I *don't* have a magic dick?" he taunts.

"Maybe you do." There's horror in my voice instead of admiration, and I think that alone is why he doesn't scoff at the comparison. "I braced myself for pain. To endure it. To fake an orgasm and give you a show that would make a good impression."

"You're saying that wasn't a show?"

"It wasn't. I would have been far more convincing otherwise." I look at him directly, but his eyes are fixed straight ahead. He's stewing over that confession, squaring it with whatever conclusions he's already come to. "I'm sure you realize that."

"I will admit that those in my harem know to crow about how big my cock is. Never to tell me to go slow. To take what I give them with a sexy little smile."

"Would you prefer if I did that?"

He laughs but doesn't rush to agree. "I desire for women to be as expected. Sexy. Sweet. Quiet. Something tells me you are only a *few* of those things, chica."

"I didn't think you'd want to see me again," I confess, hoping to change the subject.

"Don't sell yourself short now." Rather than laughter, a guttural sound resonates in his throat. "There is one thing you'll learn about me, Lupe or Tiena. Whoever you are. I love a good mystery. Nothing in the world thrills me more than seeing through a veil of bullshit to the truth lurking underneath."

I struggle to keep my expression blank. "You think I've fed you bullshit?"

"I do. I think you talk a good game, little Lupe. You lie so convincingly, that even I might have fallen for your story from the outset. Normally I don't fuck those who seek to deceive me. You have my interest. I'm curious to see what you'll do with it."

As if on cue, we arrive at our destination—an Italian-style restaurant, far more elegant than what I would expect where he is concerned. He helps me out of the car and guides me inside. In the periphery, I note at least three men who trail into the lobby after us, but when we're finally seated, it's only Jaguar and me at a table in a private dining room that overlooks a beautiful courtyard and an illuminated garden.

We're served sparkling water, wine worth more than a year of rent, and an elegant spread of appetizers.

I sample dishes at random, tasting nothing. My full attention is on the man across from me—even the best thing I've ever tasted can't compare.

To strengthen my unease, he hasn't eaten anything. He watches me instead.

"As much fun as I've had enjoying your company, Lupe, I would like to turn our discussion to business."

"Oh?"

"You said you offered yourself to me. Your soul. *But*—" He folds his hands together and sits forward. "When you make a deal with the devil, chica, he needs to know he can collect."

I nearly choke on a mouthful of salad. Grasping for a napkin, I press it to my lips and regain my senses before daring to speak. "Last night wasn't proof enough?"

I don't sound insulted. Maybe I'm not. He would not be here if he wasn't interested in me even a little. Perhaps it's as simple as he claimed—I'm a mystery he's eager to solve and then shelve.

If that's the case, I should stall until Franco is safe.

"I don't want you to doubt me, Jaguar."

"Last night earned you a favor," he clarifies. "You want to earn more? It will take a lot more than a pity fuck."

I set my fork aside and fold my hands over the table—mainly to hide how they tremble. "Such as?"

"You offered your loyalty, but forgive me if I won't take just your word for it. I need you to prove it to me."

"How?"

He sits back and inclines his head. "Do a job for me."

I don't think he's talking about bartending or bussing tables.

"I'm not well versed in your business, Jaguar. What use could you have for me?"

"Plenty," he says with a gleam in his eye. "A sexy piece of ass like you could have *plenty* of uses. What I have in mind can be done in a day. Nothing too hot, of course."

Because a man like him has a literal inferno of criminal activity under his purview. I've heard the horror stories about him and the operation he runs, the Guarida, and I'm sure they're just a fraction of what he dabbles in—drug trafficking, prostitution, extortion.

"You merely have to dip your toes into the water to prove that there is action behind the pretty words that come out of that mouth, Lupe."

It unnerves me that he still utilizes my real nickname in addition to Tiena. Despite my best efforts, I am unable to keep my expression blank. "How?"

"Do what I tell you to do. We'll discuss the particulars tomorrow. Tonight, we can continue to get acquainted." He brings a glass of wine to his lips and takes a measured sip.

A smart woman would keep her mouth shut and let him savor his supposed victory.

I can't. "Can you at least tell me why I would risk far more than having unprotected sex with a gangster by working for him?"

It's blunter than I normally talk, but being in his orbit does something to me. It strips me of the pretense I'm used to putting on around others. He commands only brutal honesty. No fluff.

"Because I know what you really want," he tells me, brandishing his wine glass in my direction. "You want your son in your arms, Braulio neutralized, and a new life far away where you can live in bliss. Am I wrong?"

I don't deny it. "And you can give me that life?"

The offer seems too good to be true, but his expression remains deadly serious.

"I can give you more, chica. More than you can imagine, but to deal with me, I need to know I can trust you."

"You can." I can't deny how tempting the carrot he's dangled before me is. It's a beautiful fantasy, but I'm willing to chase it until my dying day—whether I have to deal with Jaguar or the devil himself.

"That's a good girl." He motions for dessert, and not even an hour later, we're outside, waiting for the valet to fetch his vehicle. His smirk has vanished, but I sense that I've only momentarily placated him. There is something else he wants from me.

When we're alone in his car, I gather up the nerve to ask what.

He laughs. "You have balls, little Lupe—I will give you that. Tell me what I could possibly want from you?"

There aren't many potential options available.

"It could be sex," I say. "But you have all the women in your harem to pick from. What appeal could I possibly have?"

"All the women in my harem." Abruptly, he pulls over onto the side of the road. We're outside of the city, surrounded by trees. A bit of panic sinks in, but he's already exiting the car, approaching my end.

As he pulls my door open, he inspects me in the overhead light.

"They're all sexy as hell, down to fuck at a moment's notice. None of them can orgasm on a dime like you can, though." He snatches my wrist and yanks me out to meet him.

In anticipation of fear, I brace myself. I *should* feel it—but I don't. Even as he grips my hips and presses me into the side of the car, I feel nothing but a lightning-quick thrill shoot down my spine.

"Can you do so again?" he asks.

I feign ignorance of the crude suggestion. "What?"

A feral smile bares his teeth in a chilling flash of ivory. "Writhe on my cock, Little Lupe. Make those sexy noises like it's the best damn one you've ever felt. I must admit, I was impressed by that." Genuine curiosity creeps into his gaze. He meant that.

And my brain goes blank. I should say something encouraging, I think—feed him the sensual lies Pedro taught me. Only I can't remember them anymore. When my lips do part, the only sound to escape is a gasp.

Jaguar sighs. "Don't tell me that was a one-time trick? That's a damn shame…" His hand returns to my thigh as his fingers nudge my panties aside and sink inside me. Instantly, all logic fades.

"Oh," he says, his voice coarse. "I guess not. You're dripping for me, Lupe."

He's right. More than that. I'm reacting to him without realizing it. One touch from him, and I'm a primal animal, relying only on instinct. Spreading my legs wider to welcome him in. Bucking my hips in invitation so he can rip my panties off and slip them into his pocket.

By then, I'm already gripping the front of his slacks to hasten them down. At the back of my mind, a voice of reason screams. *What are you doing, Pita?*

Debasing myself for sex. Embodying the whore I pretended to be. Mere hours ago, the realization would have devastated me but now… Is it so wrong to get one small, selfish benefit out of this insane arrangement? When it comes to Julian Domingas, it's ironic that what I initially feared has turned out to be the most enjoyable aspect of him.

I can't breathe until I feel him inside of me. When I do, it's heaven.

I've spent so long living in hell I'd forgotten what it felt like to be free of sin. Free of worry. The man fucks all sense out of me, and I can't deny that it feels so good to forget. To moan and writhe as a stronger body slams into mine. His strength is infectious. I feel as though I could run a marathon. Sprint to California on foot. Face Diego and finally banish the ghost of him that still haunts me.

But sex with Jaguar isn't all rainbows and unicorns. It's violent, being pressed against the side of a car out in the open for the world to see. It's gnashing teeth raking at my throat hard enough to draw blood. It's a groan that revs in his chest and ripples into my ear.

"Fuck," he hisses, describing our dynamic perfectly.

It's twisted, mindless, animalistic need.

"Eager little Lupe," Jaguar growls as I meet his next punishing thrust. "You mew like a little kitten for me. Convincing enough. But can you repeat that trick?"

Without warning, he lifts me up and staggers to the back of the car, placing my ass on the trunk. Between my legs, he's massive. He takes a leg in either hand, and spreads them wider for me. Then he forces one to bend, propping it against his shoulder.

From this position, he enters me again, and the different angle heightens everything to a painful degree. His size. His firm, persistent movements.

The white-hot pleasure licking through my veins…

I'm in that hazy, dreamlike state again, on the verge of another earth-shattering feeling. It begins in my belly and crawls up my spine, tightening every muscle. My head rears back against the metal of the trunk, and I find myself staring up at him, rocking in time with every movement.

"Don't forget," he grates, grinding his pelvis into mine. "I want to see you do that trick. One. Last. Time."

Like a wind-up doll, I obey his command, and writhe mindlessly on his cock, trapped in the throes of an orgasm. This one is so relentless, it terrifies me. Above my own cries, I hear him rasp, "*Sí*, little Lupe. Just like that."

With a triumphant shout, he slams himself home, and I swear my orgasm begins all over again. It's so sharp, taking on a painful edge that has me so raw his every movement burns. Then a flood of fire washes over it and acts as a soothing balm.

When I return to my senses, Jaguar still has my thigh slung over his shoulder. He presses his lips to the flesh as I watch. Whether it's an affectionate gesture or a bold warning, I'm not sure.

"Good girl," he praises in a throaty voice. His thumb strokes along my knee, raising more devious streaks of fire. This is affection, I think. "It seems you've honed your tricks to employ them on command. You are either very talented, or…"

He trails off while wrenching me into a sitting position. With a firm tug on my skirt, he pulls it into place and then retrieves my panties from his pocket, tugging them up my legs.

"Or?" I ask once fully clothed, still breathless.

"Or someone hard to predict. I don't particularly care for the unexpected."

Uh-Oh. I try to laugh off his thinly-veiled suspicion. "Maybe you need a woman who can give you something different from your usual harem, Jaguar?"

As he heads for the car, he says nothing. *Damn it.* I can sense his interest shift, and when I join him in the passenger's seat, I decide to change the subject myself to a different topic. Business.

"What kind of job am I doing for you?"

Strangely, this unnerves me more than fucking him sans protection twice within twenty-four hours does. Sex has already been ruined by Diego. It holds no sanctity to me.

My conscience, on the other hand? That's been fairly clean relative to the life I've led. Dipping into criminal activity for Jaguar would be a new, untread territory.

As if sensing my discomfort, he inclines his head toward me and flashes his characteristic smirk.

"Oh no, Lupe. I won't spoil the surprise. I'll be around to pick you up in the morning. Ten. Be on time. You can meet me in the lobby."

He drops me off at Pedro's apartment, and I enter the building alone. After taking a long shower, and staring at myself in the mirror for even longer, I still can't figure out what has gotten into me. I should have taken the money I won and bought a plane ticket to California first thing. I should be hunting down a mercenary who can procure Franco. I should be shaking down Braulio. I should be…

Doing anything but screwing a man so dangerous, the entire world trembles at the sound of his name.

CHAPTER EIGHT

The prospect of "working" for him makes me too nervous to sleep. When morning rolls around, I text Pedro to let him know I'm okay, then I spend the rest of my time deciding what to wear. Pedro's salesgirl provided me with outfits intended for wearing while hanging from a narco's arm, not working for him.

At least in any other capacity than the obvious one.

In this one instance, however, I have a little experience of what "narco work" entails. Diego made the bulk of his money running errands for powerful men and forging his own empire in the shadows. The only use he had for women was as whores or drug mules.

Braulio is the same—even I once worked for him, though unwillingly.

Could Jaguar have a similar use in mind for me? In the end, I quell my curiosity by getting dressed and settle on a modest gray dress with short sleeves and a low pair of black heels. My hair, I arrange in the typical bun, and I enter the lobby ready for whatever I might face.

The first surprise is that Jaguar isn't who comes for me. I don't recognize the man in the front seat of a luxury sedan, but he greets me with a nod and gestures for me to take the seat beside him.

"Morning, Ms. Sanchez," he says. "Mr. Domingas sends you his blessings."

I try not to hear a threat in the greeting.

"Can I ask what he has in mind exactly?"

The man shoots me a look that warns I won't be getting any answers from him.

"Enjoy the drive, Miss. We will arrive at our destination momentarily."

Trips into the unknown are hard to enjoy. Reassuringly, we don't venture far beyond the city, but I don't recognize the area we wind up in. It seems classy, with high-priced buildings that mainly contain offices.

When the driver finally parks before one of the tallest buildings, I'm not sure what to expect. For him to hand me a ski mask and a gun to rob the place?

Instead, he gives me a business card.

"You have an appointment with this man in ten minutes. Mr. Domingas does not appreciate lateness. You are to ask for the usual transfer of accounts. The most important part?

If you notice anything odd, you report it to me, and therefore you report it to Mr. Domingas. Understood?"

When I nod, the man exits the car to open the door on my end.

The building itself looks like a fancy extension of a bank—but not the average local branch. This is where men with real money deal. Somewhere even Braulio wouldn't dare set foot.

But why send me?

There aren't many explanations I can think of. None that a man like Jaguar couldn't take care of himself or via someone far more capable than me. Therefore, this is clearly a test.

Focus Pita. I can't let myself be rattled. Clearing my head of all distractions, I follow the name on the business card and soon find myself ushered inside a massive corner office. Behind a wide desk sits a man who looks like the stereotypical accountant. He's white with neatly coifed brown hair and blue eyes that shift uneasily behind the wire frames of his glasses.

"You must be Ms. Sanchez," he says, standing to shake my hand. "Our mutual friend warned me of your visit. As you will soon see, everything is in order. There is no reason for Mr. Domingas to have any concerns."

He gestures to a row of documents lying on the desk. They appear to be various legal documents at first glance. Why would Jaguar want me to see this?

Then it hits me. Tiena wasn't all ass and tits. In between shopping excursions, she did at least one job for Braulio that made her useful enough to keep around for as long as he did.

She knew numbers like the back of her hand. She could do them in her head like a calculator, but her real trick was finding logical ways to fudge them. A missed decimal point here. A stray zero there. Even the most complex accounts could be given the appearance of legitimacy by her.

The strange part is that few people know that. Just Braulio and his most-trusted goons. And, of course, her dead sister Lupita. Unfortunately, I didn't inherit her skill, and it all seems like a foreign language to me.

Either Jaguar's decided to test if I really am Tiena, or he has another aim in mind. Perhaps he wants to see if I'll be as forthright with him as she was with her other lover?

Damn.

Damn.

Damn.

"You can take your time," the accountant says, reaching for another file that must be unconnected to whatever Jaguar wants me to see.

Sweat drips down my neck as I scan the desk and spy a picture of a beautiful family posing before a large house. They even have the customary white-picket fence and matching dog. Jealousy seeps through me. I would give anything to live so blissfully unaware of the hell the world contains.

But I am not so lucky. Resigned to my fate, I thumb through the first pile of documents, but I don't see anything strange in the calculations I can decipher. So, I reach for another page. Then another.

In theory, perhaps all is fine and well, and Jaguar merely wanted to rub in my face how much he owns. Various properties and assets—more than I could have ever imagined one man possessing. He could just want to show off. Reinforce how dangerous and powerful he is.

But as I begin to flip through the third stack of documents, I note something that has nothing to do with the numbers printed on the page.

The accountant gets antsy. Despite his efforts to appear calm, I can see the anxiety bubbling beneath. Every time I turn a page, he shifts in his seat, and gradually my focus shifts to him. Tiena had her numbers, but my skill was far more nuanced. I was always good at seeing through bullshit. I wasn't born with that talent, of course—I earned it the hard way through trial and error. In other words, Diego beat that intuition into me piece by piece. I have him to thank for finally understanding why Jaguar really sent me here.

Time doesn't even allow for second-guessing. After closing the latest file, I face the accountant and decide to make a bold guess, consequences be damned.

"How long have you been skimming from him?" I ask.

"What?" he sputters, his face reddening. Shock alone isn't the reason—I know utter terror when I see it. "I don't know what—"

"But the thievery isn't why you're sweating in a room with the air conditioning on full blast," I add, cutting him off. "You're afraid of something else."

And if there is one emotion I know inside and out, it's fear. He reeks of it, and I wonder if this is what Jaguar feels when he sees through enemies and cuts them down to the quick. Exhilarating is an understatement.

"You ratted him out, didn't you?" I ask to twist the knife.

"I'm sorry." He rushes to his feet, swiping his documents into a haphazard pile. "You should go."

I don't move. "How long have you been feeding the feds his books?"

The man holds my stare for a long time. "I have a family," he says finally. "A family he will kill if he even thinks I've done anything wrong. Turn around. Leave my office, and I will have one hundred grand wired to a foreign bank account with your name on it. Please. You have no idea what kind of man he is."

Escape is tempting, I can't deny it—but men like Jaguar value loyalty far more than any amount of money could ever buy. Neither would the word of some new sex toy be enough leverage against his personal accountant. I would need proof. But how to get it?

Pedro has his contacts. Maybe he could help.

"I think I'll take my chances. Have a good day," I tell the man before leaving his office with a file in my grasp.

The poor bastard doesn't even have the heart to stop me. I risk taking a detour into a bathroom where I call Pedro. Thank God, he answers on the first ring.

"I'm sending you pictures of some documents," I say, aware that I'm rapidly running out of time. "See if you can verify the numbers for me and find anything suspicious. Oh, and if I don't get around to it, I know where Franco is. Somewhere in California. I'll send you the pictures when I can."

"Wait, Pita—"

I hang up, too rattled to explain any further. My fingers shake like hell as I snap pics of each document in the folder I stole and send them to Pedro. When I return to the car, I pause to shove the file into my purse before greeting the driver with a nod.

"Anything out of the ordinary to report?" he asks.

"No," I say.

"Good." Either the man has an impenetrable poker face, or there was no overarching test. By the time I make it back to my borrowed apartment, I'm not sure what to think.

In any case, it's a rookie mistake to not expect the unexpected.

When I enter the living room and find Jaguar seated on the couch, wine glass in hand, I know I shouldn't be surprised.

He seems rather at home, with one foot propped on the coffee table. He's swapped his black shirt for a leather jacket worn with nothing else beneath.

"*Salud*, Lupe," he grates as I approach. "I trust you had an easy time."

"Yes, thank you," I reply, sitting on the loveseat across from him. "I will admit that was far tamer than what I had in mind."

"Was it?" His laugh upends my heart rate. That time, I clearly noted the danger openly lurking in it. "That remains to be seen. Have a drink." He offers me an already-full glass, and that uneasy feeling grows.

"Drink," he prompts.

I take a sip, impressed by the taste. It's a beautiful vintage with nothing odd in the flavor that I can discern. Yet, his eyes have that gleam again. The cat-got-the-mouse one he wore while watching the cage fight. In response to it, a little voice in my head whispers, *You're in danger, Lupe.*

Suddenly, I want to dump the entire contents of this glass down the drain. Instead, I force myself to take another sip.

"You met my accountant, Ronaldo?" Jaguar asks without drinking from his own glass. "Nice man. For five years, he's worked for me with no incident. I take it he was good to you?"

I nod. "Yes. He showed me some documents."

I can't resist running a finger along the strap of my purse. It's dangerous to withhold information from him—but taunting him with vague suspicions seems to be a far more perilous alternative.

"And did you notice anything out of the ordinary?" he asks.

My heart skips a beat. "S-Should I have?"

He laughs without answering. "I didn't ask you that. *Did you?*"

"I wouldn't burden you with suspicion or gossip," I say smoothly.

And I won't make a fool of myself by condemning a man to death without hard figures. Diego operated on impulse and suspicion. I won't do the same.

Once I get the proof from Pedro, I'll share what I know.

"Ah, that's what I like about you, Lupe," he says. "Always one with the pretty words but prone to dancing around the heart of the issue. Drink up."

I obey, only now I note that something is definitely off. My limbs feel heavier. My breath tastes sweeter. Almost as if…

"I'll give you one last piece of advice, Lupe, for what it's worth," Jaguar murmurs as my eyelids grow heavy and begin to dip. "When I warn you not to bullshit me, you take that into consideration as though your life depends on it. Chances are… It does."

CHAPTER NINE

My head is splitting. It hurts so badly that I dread having to open my eyes at all—but the smell makes me.

A gag rips from my throat, and I'm thankful my stomach is empty. God, this stench. It's rancid and sour, well beyond any stink a human could make. To compare it, I can only use the farm near where I grew up as a frame of reference. It's an odor reminiscent of dog or cow shit, but ten times worse.

Am I in a sewer?

No. The air is too cool. Air-conditioned. Then, I hear it. A low, unsettling rumble resonates through my very bones, a bit like thunder, only way more substantive. Laughter echoes above it, followed by a voice I instantly recognize.

"Wake up, Tiena," Jaguar calls. "Rise and shine."

His voice alone compels me to ignore the pain and obey his command. *Rise.* Groaning, I peel my eyes open. It's bright wherever I am, and it's dark. I'm in a puddle of illumination, but a wall of shadows obscures anything beyond it—such as the man coaching me from sight unseen.

"Wake up," he commands. "Good. Get to know your new roommates for a short while."

I'm lying on my back, and it takes effort to roll onto my side. A few realizations sink in, adding a chilling backdrop to the danger I've already picked up on. The paramount concern—I'm in a cage. It's crudely made of iron bars, clearly designed for a human. There is enough space to sit upright, but I doubt I could fully stand.

The second thing of note is that I'm not alone in this contraption. A row of iron bars separates me from a man lying on his side. I recognize him, and another pang of terror runs through me.

He's the accountant.

"Ronaldo here was just explaining to me why he traded immunity for handing over my accounts to the feds on a silver platter. Immunity." Jaguar laughs. "I don't think that was anywhere near a fair trade."

I still can't see him, but his voice is coming from somewhere ahead of me. Others mingle with his, and I'm reminded of the cage-fighting arena. This has a similar barbaric feel to it.

Humiliation on display.

I imagine that Jaguar is seated in the front row with a clear view of whatever show he expects to see.

"I'll give you the courtesy of seeing in action what happens to those who seek to betray me, Lupe," he continues. "Then you'll have to take your punishment as well for disappointing me, chica. I hope you can spin those pretty words to save your life. Gatita!"

A shrill whistle rings out, and the accountant springs into motion, gripping the bars of his cage. His glasses are askew, his suit jacket gone. A bloodied nose gives the impression that he had a private meeting with Jaguar before I woke up. "Please, Jaguar. I have a family. They threatened my wife. I had no choice! Please—"

"Family?" A figure steps from the shadows, his head cocked smugly, his eyes blazing. Jaguar. "We are all family here," he snarls. "If you go against me, you go against us all. I am your family, and this is what happens to those who forsake that loyalty—" His eyes cut to somewhere behind us, and he smiles. "Let her in. Ah, there she is, my little Gatita. Come see what treats Daddy has brought you. Ah, my sweet baby. Come. Come."

Terrifying noises erupt in the wake of his command. A door opening with a metal creak. Scratching sounds. A quiet thud. As the sounds grow louder, I note the concrete floor beneath me is damp with a dark substance. It's the source of the smell, rancid and sticky. Something far thicker than water, and even in the dark, I can tell it's red.

Numb with dread, I peek over my shoulder and discover the source of Jaguar's excitement.

A large feline slinks from the shadows near the back of the room, strikingly similar to the one tattooed on his bicep. An *actual* jaguar blacker than night. Despite his loving nickname of "kitty" in Spanish, this animal is anything but a juvenile. On powerful hind limbs, it bounds to the cage and bats the row of bars nearest to the cowering accountant.

Clang!

The man shrieks and scrambles toward my end, separated from me by another set of rigid bars. His eyes are so wide I see myself reflected in them. A stupid, foolish idiot who just gave her life away.

"My baby was sleeping in her private room, but she's never too sleepy for a snack. Any last words, Ronaldo?" Jaguar asks above the former's whimpering. "No? I guess you want to get better acquainted with my little girl, here. Who am I to stop you?" He raises his hand, revealing a remote in his fist. He must press a button because the metal grate on Ronaldo's side of the cage begins to rise. Eagerly, the jaguar rakes its paws beneath the opening while the accountant shrieks and presses himself against the barrier between us.

It's no use.

The second the grate is high enough, the beast lunges.

Oh, God. A desperate need to turn away starts to enter my mind, but I resist at the last minute. Diego used to parade his horrific actions in front of me from time to time. He shot a man once. Electrocuted one, too. For sport, he tortured plenty of dogs by making them fight in the ring. No matter the nature of the display, I quickly learned the best method to survive them all intact.

The most important lesson? Never shy from violence. To him, any show of fear was always taken as an invitation to increase his cruelty.

Second was to communicate with him. Speak. He wanted to lord his viciousness over me but talking to keep him tethered—made him less likely to escalate his actions.

So I talk now, fighting to raise my voice above the accountant's screams. What I'm witnessing isn't like in the movies. The animal doesn't go for his jugular for a nice clean kill.

It latches those massive jaws onto his thigh instead. Then it begins to drag him…

I'll be next if I don't do something. *Focus, Pita!*

"What have I done to upset you, Jaguar?" I manage to croak. Somehow my voice doesn't break. I sound too calm. Unfazed. "Tell me."

He laughs, and I risk swiveling around to face him, looping one hand through the bars.

"Either you were too dumb to see his shoddy work, or you deliberately lied to me," he says. "I've heard the rumors, Tiena. You're supposed to be good with numbers. You should have spotted the mistakes. Why didn't you?"

So, he knew of my sister's trick after all. *Damn it.* I can't think of a good lie in this moment. Though, trying to trick him at all could backfire. Left with no other option, I improvise.

"Tell you a hunch without evidence? Feed you a suspicion?"

My voice does break then. A crunching sound makes me glance over my shoulder, and I instantly regret it. It's a scene that will haunt me for eternity. I can't even describe it in full. Blood and crunching bone. Through it all, Ronaldo screams and screams.

Oh, God…

"Suspicion, chica?" Jaguar parrots. Fighting down a wave of bile, I turn back to him and blink to bring him into clarity. *Focus, Pita.* "I wanted you to be honest with me," he growls. "You kept quiet and let a hornet remain in my nest."

"No," I counter, gripping both bars so tightly my knuckles whiten. "I needed to corroborate. Why bring you half-assed reasoning? I know the risk to those who betray you. I wanted to make sure."

"And how would you do that?"

I hesitate. Revealing more could expose Pedro to danger. How to do so without dragging his name into it?

"I needed to clarify," I say thickly. "The numbers were wrong, but what does that mean?"

"It means, he was selling me out, Lupe—"

"*No.*" I smack the bars separating us for emphasis. "It means there could be more out there you don't know. He took money off the top, but men like that aren't stupid. He hid some, I'm sure, even from the feds. Don't you want to know what it is? Or who could have been paying him?"

Jaguar smiles and begins to clap, loudly and slowly. "And here it is, ladies and gentlemen. In addition to a magic pussy, this chica's got a magic tongue."

"Perhaps I'm the only one who's been honest to you," I snap back without bothering to feign politeness. "Honest enough to avoid leading you to act impulsively."

"Then be honest with me, now," he says, stepping forward.

I draw a deep breath. This lighting wreaks havoc over his unique features, casting shadows where his eyes should be. He looks like a demon, hungry for blood. More alarming, he looks far too insane to reach through logic.

"Beg for forgiveness and plead for your life," he demands. "Maybe I'll rethink my plans for you."

"No." Judging from the sudden lack of cries, I think the jaguar is done with Ronaldo. It will turn to me next, and a fight or flight instinct rips through me so violently I shake. *Run,* my brain screams. Keeping my back to the creature is foolish, but I sense that I have no choice.

When Diego tired of his little display, he always made me face him. *What now, Pita, my little butterfly? You think I'm a piece of shit. Say it!*

I would have to lie, of course. Tell him how strong he was. How invincible. How fearsome."

In this instance, I don't do either.

"I won't insult you by groveling," I say, sounding calm once again. "If you think I deserve to die, then kill me now. I won't beg. If you believe I failed you, then I deserve to die—"

Metal clangs behind me, and I don't react quickly enough. Wham! A heavy force slams into my hip as fire rakes across my back. In the face of it, I make the second biggest mistake of my life besides meeting Jaguar in the first place. I scream.

God, it hurts, and I imagine myself being ripped apart by those claws, and teeth.

It takes all of my focus to keep talking. For all I know, they could be my last words. I take one small, shred of pride in the fact that I don't regret saying them. "Go ahead and kill me. I won't insult you by begging."

My vision blurs, obscuring my view of him. At my back, the metal continues to rattle. Clang. A stomach-churning stench washes over me, tinged with heat. Gatita's breath. One more hit, and she'll rip me open, then gorge on the remains…

"Ah, that's enough." That high-pitched whistle sounds again, and I sense the entire cage rock and rattle with the jaguar's retreat. "Enough, Gatita."

Still in my view, Jaguar himself advances and raises the remote. The bars in front of me shift and begin to lift, but I don't move. Not until he stops paces away, and inclines his head.

"Your magic tongue works again, chica. Horatio!" He gestures toward someone out of my view. "Take Lupe to clean up, then bring her to my suite. Show's over *pendejos*."

He exits the space first, disappearing through that veil of shadow. In his place, another man steps forward.

He must be Horatio—a balding man with a scar cutting through his left eye. Unceremoniously, he yanks me to my feet and leads me away from the cage. I wasn't far off in judging that this arena was similar to the one at the club. It's smaller, however, and surrounded by assorted pieces of leather furniture on which various members of Jaguar's entourage lounge.

They eye me warily, but I can't see straight. My back is on fire, and something warm and wet is dribbling down my thigh. I feel like I'm melting.

"This way," a voice snaps as I falter. A firm grip holds me upright and manhandles me down a darkened hallway.

I'm as weak as if I've walked for miles though it must only be a few feet before I'm shoved into a spacious bathroom.

"Sit."

Horacio nods toward a toilet with the lid down.

He rummages through the cupboards while I try my hardest to regain control of my breathing. More blood is pouring out of me than I've ever seen in one place. Too much. I'll die if this keeps up. Die.

No! I pinch my wrist until a semblance of clarity returns to my thoughts. I'm panicking, and I can't afford to now. *Damn it. Focus, Pita.*

After all, this isn't the worst I've been through. Not by a long shot.

One time Diego hurt me bad. So badly, I had to go to the hospital under an assumed name and was there a week for monitoring. The pain in this instance is no different from that. I need to stay focused. Keep breathing. Don't scream.

"Ah." Horacio prods my lower back. "These are superficial, but this one is deep. You move—it will hurt. I won't waste the good stuff on you, but here—" He shoves a bottle into my hand. It's brown liquor.

I recall the last time I drank something and try to give it back.

"Drink it," he warns. "It's straight tequila. You'll need it."

"I don't need anything," I rasp with a familiar weariness in my voice. "Just get it over with."

"Doctor's not here," the man says gruffly though he withdraws the bottle. "I stitch you myself. It will hurt."

I say nothing.

True to his word, the old man cleans my wounds and then leaves for a heartbeat before returning with a battered metal case from which he draws a medical needle and black thread. He applies stitches to the deepest puncture mark, and tears stream down my face by the time he's done. I don't look back, but I suspect there are five in total.

With a satisfied grunt, Horatio tosses a bloodied rag aside and heads for the door.

"Come," he calls back to me. "He wants you in his suite."

I don't know how I manage to stand, let alone walk properly. Jaguar's suite is down a long winding hallway and up a flight of stairs. It's large and spacious, decorated in shades of black. A window overlooks a familiar scene—the pool I glimpsed the first time I was in Jaguar's mansion—but viewed from another angle.

"That was a beautiful show, chica."

I turn to find Jaguar loping into the room like his predatory namesake—only this time, the comparison isn't figurative. My heart races. A familiar sensation churns down my spine, and I welcome it like an old friend. Fear. After viewing the cruelty he is capable of, Julian Domingas has become a familiar monster I've faced countless times before—but he doesn't even measure up to the real thing. Diego has done far worse to me than trying to feed me to an animal.

Far, far worse.

"I'm glad you enjoyed it," I croak. Adrenaline alone makes for one hell of a drug. I don't feel a damn thing though I know I should be writhing in agony. I must be delirious. Or insane. Whatever infects me, I'm grateful as hell for it as it gives me the strength to incline my head and meet his stare head-on. "Next time, you should aim to draw more blood. It will better satisfy those sharks you keep at your beck and call, and a nastier scar makes for a far better war story to tell."

Don't I know it. Diego, for all the violence he inflicted on my body, was rather stingy when it came to the marks left behind to remember him by. My collection of scars is small but grisly. I look at them and shudder every single time. In my nightmares, I relive the infliction of each one, and they feel as real as the day he made them. Oh yes, Jaguar is off to a rousing start, but even this doesn't come close.

I tell myself that over and over. *It doesn't.* I've survived worse —I can survive this. I will survive him.

"Your magic tongue gets sharp when you're angry," Jaguar scolds. He crosses to a mini bar in the corner of the room and pours himself a shot of whiskey. Rather than drink it, he spins the liquid in its glass and eyes me from over the rim. "Have a drink. Have a seat. Let's discuss this proof you planned to gather for me."

A ragged sound rips out of me that I barely recognize. A laugh. A genuine one. "Oh, but I've already failed you, *Jaguar*," I say, rolling the moniker around my tongue. It's rude as hell, but I don't feel one ounce of regret. Instead, I feel hysterical. I'm high on pain after years of withdrawal. I'm even smiling as I face him with dried blood still encrusted on my skin. "I won't dare insult you by lingering to remind you of that shame. I'll be leaving now. Give Gatita my warmest regards."

"Oh no, Lupe." He chuckles, shaking his head. Then he downs his shot in one go and pours another. "You aren't going anywhere. Do you understand? You owe a debt to me, chica. From now on, you don't do shit unless I tell you to. You don't leave unless I grant you permission. You won't even take a shit unless I allow you to. *Claro?*"

"You think you can control me?" The taunt is out before I can bite it back. The scary part? I don't want to. I square my chin and stand ten toes down in the rebellious rage creeping beneath my skin.

"I don't control you," he says, his eyes unreadable. "I own you."

A tendril of unease runs down my battered spine. He's saying all the right things, but his tone is off. He's too angry. There's none of that violent, wild instability that warns he means every word. He's not interested in me enough to put fire behind those threats. This is him merely going through the motions.

And some of my resolve cracks. I'm used to facing down a full-throated monster. Not a bored one.

"I respect you, Jaguar," I tell him. Maybe I even do. "But don't waste your time playing with a toy you don't want. It demeans us both. Thank you for a wonderful evening, but—"

"Did I say you could fucking move?"

Because I've already started for the doorway. In the face of his growled statement, I keep walking. The fact that he grabs me isn't a surprise, but the tension in his grip is. It hurts, but not hard enough to bruise. Again, I'm just getting a taste of his frustration. He's holding back. Why?

It doesn't matter. No longer does he intrigue me.

When I wrench out of his grasp, he lets me go, and I don't look back.

"I am willing to subject myself to many things, but mind games isn't one of them," I tell him. "You want a little whore who will jump through your hoops and cower, go take your pick from your harem. I always mean what I say, and I told you that you had me. If you don't trust that, then we have nothing left to discuss. I don't chase after men who aren't interested in what I have to offer."

"Oh, I beg to differ, Tiena," he growls. "Word on the street is that you're an insatiable slut, and you'll do anything and anyone for a new purse and some pretty shoes. Your devoted mother ruse is convincing, but don't fool yourself."

I look back at him, and I almost regret it. It would help somewhat if he resembled how Diego would look in this instance. Furious. Enraged. A beast out for blood.

Jaguar merely looks amused. I'm not living up to his expectations, and it thrills him. It puzzles him. Curiosity makes his gaze more searing than ever, as if he hopes to burn whatever secrets I'm hiding out of my skull.

"If you want me to get your son, then you'll do whatever the fuck I tell you to—"

"No," I say, lifting my chin. "I am not a toy to sit on a shelf with your other dolls. You're bored of me, Jaguar. You like your women cowering and fearful, but I don't fear anyone."

Not anymore.

Infected by my newfound boldness, I keep going, "I appreciate your help, but as I told you before, if you won't help me, I'll find someone who will. Now give me my phone and have a lovely night."

"You really think you can walk away from me?"

I don't let myself falter a single step in my third quest for the door. "Yes," I say with my back to him. "If you wanted me for real, we wouldn't be having this conversation. Now enough with the dangerous man spiel. I know exactly how your kind operates, and I know a windup when I hear it."

Does it bother him to have those words thrown in his face? It does.

"Goodnight."

I keep moving, but I don't hear any footsteps in my wake. Good. I force myself onward until a wide-eyed woman passes me and warily points toward the front entrance.

When I exit the main doors under the gaze of a watchman, a car is waiting for me out front. Inside it, I find my purse and my cell phone in the back seat. Only when I safely reach my apartment—somehow avoiding the view of anyone who might notice my torn dress—do I try to call Pedro.

I barely let it ring once before hanging up. Instead, I strip my dress and climb into the shower. The hot water lashes at my back, awakening the pain that remained dormant until now.

Only in the sanctity of the stall can I finally scream and cry and writhe beneath the agony. I don't despair over it. I wallow in it and cherish the strength pain gives me. It's a rush of a far stronger drug than adrenaline. It's a cruel reminder of everything I've survived up until this point.

In a poetic sense, Lupita Sanchez is dead, and a phoenix rose from her ashes. Never again will a powerful man have me under his thumb, no more loved than a disposable piece of trash.

Not Diego.

Not Braulio Rivera.

Not Julian Domingas.

When I finally exit the shower, I find at least ten missed calls from the only man I can trust, Pedro.

"You stupid bitch," he scolds when I finally call him back. "Don't you ever fucking scare me like that. *Dios mío*. I ought to kick your skinny ass back to Mexico. What was so important you had to ignore your phone for twelve hours?"

"Pedro…" I bite my lip so hard it stings just to hold back a sob. I can't tell him the truth. Not because he wouldn't understand—if anyone would, it's Pedro. *He*, not Tiena, was the one who helped lick my wounds and bandage my bloodied limbs. He helped resurrect the corpse of my old self Diego had left behind. He knows the risks that come with associating with dangerous men.

So no, I can't tell him.

"Pita? What the hell happened?"

"I got held up. Did you do what I asked?"

It's funny how I can focus on that and sound somewhat normal. It's time to stop bitching. Franco is all that matters.

"The number stuff? Yeah. Or did you mean Francisco? I came by last night, but you weren't here. Still, I took the liberty of tracking that house in the picture you had. It's somewhere in Calabasas. Nice place. As for the other stuff, I left it on the coffee table, but Pita, what the hell is going on with you and Jaguar? Did you score him again—"

"I don't want to talk about him. I need a ticket on a private plane or whatever the hell you can get me on. I need to be in California tomorrow. Can you help me, Pedro?"

"Mamacita, you're scaring me. You sound strange. Like you're high. Don't tell me Jaguar had you sample his merchandise."

"No, but listen to me, Pedro. I need a way out. Please."

"Okay, Pita. I'm on it. But I'm going to start charging interest sooner or later. You are one expensive bitch. Oh, and don't forget the number stuff is in the living room. Use it wisely, Pita. That was a very big favor to call in. I also had some copies of Tiena's IDs made. Enjoy them while you can. I have to go. Ciao."

He hangs up, and I call him back, only to get a busy tone. I don't doubt that he'll come through, but I'm anxious to go now. Fly now. Get to California now. Run now. Get as far from Jaguar as I can.

The last thing I should want to do is confirm my hunch about his numbers. Still, I find myself limping into the living room to discover the pile of documents Pedro left for me to find. As it turns out, I was right. Jaguar's accountant was doing far more than just skimming off the top. I recognize the carefully arranged lump sums. I'm not an expert in calculations like Tiena, but I do know a thing or two about spotting theft. Diego was renowned for his caution—especially after he caught one of his men taking outside payments and using clever property buys to hide the excess.

Ronaldo had been paid off by someone who wasn't Jaguar. But why? And for what purpose?

A woman loyal to him would try to find out or perhaps use the knowledge as leverage to get in his good graces.

Like hell will I.

I shove the papers aside and wind up on the couch. I don't want it to happen, the sobbing. But it does, in slow snatches at first. Then a torrent.

Just like that, I'm decades in the past, stuck in an apartment half the size of this one. I can't freely come and go as I choose. My entire life is dictated by one man's whims. His actions decide my every reaction. He is my world, my universe, my god.

I owe him everything, and the mere second I forget that, he'll take the last thing I have.

My life, if not my very soul.

CHAPTER TEN

I don't know how in the hell I managed to sleep, but I needed it. My head feels clearer, and I almost forget that I was mauled by an exotic animal last night at the whim of a homicidal psychopath.

Almost.

When I attempt to stand, my back burns like hell, and I curl into a ball, afraid to move for God knows how long. When I finally do drag myself upright, it's early morning with snatches of sunlight licking at the windows. Good. I have an entire day of planning ahead of me. Just how quickly can I get my ass to California?

I will do whatever it takes to find out.

Pedro is a saint. I check my phone to find that he got me a last-minute flight to California that leaves in the afternoon. It's not as soon as I would like, but it's today, at least. A start. I don't have anything to pack, and my fake documents are in my purse. I limp toward it to refresh my memory of the false identity, only to trip over a folder of stray documents, scattering them over the floor.

Getting to Francisco should dominate my thoughts, and it does… Lurking beside him, where he doesn't belong, however, is a man who haunts me still. I could leave for California, but he'll follow, always in my head. Unlike Diego, he didn't earn his place there. My fascination with the bastard itches, uncomfortable and unwelcome.

The only way to drive him out is to end this "bargain" on my terms. As luck would have it, there is just enough time to do so if I hurry.

Maybe it's a testament to how stupid I know this plan is deep down, but I don't call Pedro for advice. He'd just talk me out of this insanity—but it's been a long time since I've embodied crazy Pita. Without an ounce of uncertainty, I grab one of my new dresses from the floor and find a pair of scissors in the kitchen. My final outfit isn't one my friend would approve of, but, wearing it, I don't feel like a narco's arm candy.

I feel like me. Lupita back from the dead with one last act of vengeance to carry out—confront a new monster before he can overtake the scars left by the old one.

Minutes later, I call a car service and head to an address I've learned by heart. When I arrive, it isn't the welcoming paradise brimming with sexy young women that I've been presented with. It's a fortress, guarded by armed men who patrol the front yard and eye me skeptically. The front gates don't magically part for me, either. I must exit the car and address a stern-faced man who demands my purpose.

"To see Jaguar," I say.

He steps away and barks into a cell phone while inspecting my appearance. From the neck up, I look the part of dumb, pretty arm candy. My outfit, however, tarnishes that image —I'm wearing a beautiful mini-dress with the back crudely cut out to reveal jagged, open wounds for anyone to see.

I think they're even bleeding, aggravated by my trip here.

A minute later, the guard nods to beckon me inside, and the driver drops me off before the paved walkway leading to the front door. Viewed in the daylight, it's a fiery path to Hell, and I follow it without hesitation.

The front door isn't locked, and I boldly open it rather than knock. The doorman isn't here, neither is the rest of Jaguar's entourage. Odd. Does he only parade them around when he knows an audience will be watching? The prospect serves to do the opposite of what I hoped to accomplish by coming here—he's even more interesting than before.

A narco who only plays the part? Or a man who trusts in his reputation so much he fears no one, enough to let strange women into his home unaccompanied…

Julian Domingas is quite the enigma.

Somehow, I know exactly where he'll be—in a pink bedroom near his suite, on a massive bed with three naked bimbos draped over his body. When I toe the threshold, he doesn't seem surprised. Even though his eyes remain closed, his lip twitches into that trademark smirk. I stiffen. Did he expect me to come?

No, I think. That's why he's so amused. "Lupe." He inclines an eyebrow without lifting his head from a mound of silken pillows. "To what do I owe this visit? Did you want to see my harem in action, perhaps? You've missed the show, I'm afraid." His laugh would make a weaker woman blush with shame. I just stare, refusing to take my eyes off him, even as his companions begin to stir.

"By the way," Jaguar adds, opening his eyes, "your pussy may be magic, but nothing beats a nice big ass you can grab onto—" He slaps the ass of the nearest blond for emphasis, and she moans and rolls over. He's naked as well, unshielded by the covers. Aware of where my gaze darts, he grins. "Did you care to join us for round two?"

"No. Like you, I always pay my debts. You want to know that you have my loyalty?" I raise the crumpled folder in my grasp. "Here. The information on our friend Ronaldo that I wanted to bring you in full."

He smirks. "As if I don't already know the full story, chica."

He has no reason to lie, but I still feel the need to say, "Like that he was being *paid* to skim off the top from you?"

His eyes narrow. "Ah, the magic tongue returns. I hope this isn't a 'suspicion' that you can't back up, Lupe."

"It's all in here." I throw the folder onto the bed. "The bastard was hiding the money right under your nose while selling you out. Someone put him up to it. At least you can rest easy knowing that he deserved to face your 'punishment.' As for me? Well, our bargain is now neatly ended. I thank you for the souvenirs."

I turn on my heel to leave.

"Wait."

I look back to find him attempting to stand. He shoves a brunette off of him. "All of you. Get the fuck out. Now."

Groaning, his bedmates scramble from the room, leaving me alone with him. Fully naked, Jaguar positions himself on the edge of the mattress and snatches my folder. It isn't long into his perusal of the first few pages that his entire expression changes.

Flashing with mistrust, his eyes cut to mine. "Where the hell did you get this?"

"I told you I needed to be sure," I say, refusing to so much as flinch. "Had you given me more than a few minutes to make a judgment, I could have had all of this to you well before my meeting with Gatita." I sound bitter. Good. I am.

"But *where* did you get it from?" He spins to face me directly, an eyebrow raised. "I hope you haven't been waving my numbers around for the world to see, Lupe."

"I got my suspicions confirmed by concrete intel," I say, evading the accusation. "And if I truly wanted to betray you, I wouldn't need to show those numbers to the whole world. I would track down whoever has been paying off Ronaldo. I'm sure it's someone powerful enough to take such a bold risk. Had you waited, you could have asked before feeding him to your pet."

"Careful, Lupe," he scolds in a tone laced with warning. "You've just revealed yourself to be a threat to me. Perhaps I should feed you to my kitty as well?"

Pain is one hell of a drug—I don't even react to the threat.

"Or, you could have taken me up on my first offer," I feel tempted to say. "You could have trusted me, and I would have uncovered this sooner."

"Trust a woman purely on her juicy pussy and pretty words? Oh no, Lupe, you aren't that naïve. You're desperate as hell —" He sits back, stroking his thumb along his chin. "I think you need to give me another reason to keep you on my side."

"I'm the only one with a good damn reason to be on your side," I say. "Give me what I want, and you have no reason to ever fear betrayal from me."

He laughs. "You make it sound so easy, Lupe, but shall I reiterate just what you want? Braulio Rivera dead. That is no small ask."

"No. I just want—"

"Enough with the fucking lies!" He throws the folder aside, sending the documents scattering. I have enough sense to back away—but just a step. I could never run fast enough if he truly wanted to hurt me.

"You aren't a fool," he growls. "You know that what you want won't come easy. Your son in your arms and a new life freed from the shadow of your ex-lover. Oh yes, Lupe. You want the bastard dead and gone, and I'll tell you now that it will cost you a lot damn more than sex and boasts. Can you handle that? I suggest you think carefully."

"There is nothing to think over," I reply with a shrug. The simple motion strains my back, and it hurts so badly I could scream. I have to suck in air just to say, "As I told you, if you won't help me, I'll find someone who will. Now, if you excuse me, I have a plane to catch."

"And if I were to send you to Braulio in a body bag? I think he might pay handsomely for that. Far more than you can afford, chica."

"Do it." It scares me how cold my voice sounds, devoid of fear. It's the old Lupita talking. The girl who flirted with death daily and barely lived to tell the tale. "I'll even save you the trouble of procuring a body bag. Learn one thing about me, Jaguar, if nothing at all—I don't fear death. Not in the slightest. You know what *does* frighten me? Having my time wasted by mind games and useless party tricks."

I've lost so much ground already.

"Have a wonderful morning," I add while starting for the door. "If I see your harem girls on the way out, I'll send them back in—"

"Wait. It seems as though we've gotten off on the wrong foot, Lupe." His voice dips, but the tone is far warmer than I'm used to. Suddenly, he's cordial.

And I'm suspicious.

"Let's reacquaint ourselves over breakfast on me," he suggests.

"No," I blurt before I have enough sense to tack on, "I have a flight to catch."

"And I have a home in California with your name on it should you play your cards right," he counters. "*Claro?*"

I bite my lower lip. *Damn him.* He could be bluffing. But…

Pedro can only do so much. Once I make it to California, I'll be on my own, forced to hunt for Francisco alone. Forced to contend with Braulio's security detail alone.

"Ah, it seems you need more convincing," Jaguar says, audibly disappointed. "I'll even call my doctor to look at your back and give you something to take the edge off."

"I have my own doctor," I lie. Like hell will I allow anyone in his employ to come near me with a mind-altering substance. "And I'm not in the mood for breakfast. We can talk, but I am a busy woman Jaguar as I am sure you are a busy man. We should make it quick."

"You sure do enjoy testing my patience," he warns, rising to his feet. "Hand me that robe over there."

He nods to a bit of black silk slung over a leather chair beside the window. I toss it to him, and he takes his sweet time covering himself with it.

Then he presses a button affixed to the wall near the bed. "My guest will be staying for breakfast," he says into it. "Prepare the dining room. We aren't to be disturbed."

A meek voice comes through an unseen intercom in response, "Yes, Sir."

Jaguar turns to me. "Be a good girl and wait for me." He nods to the hallway. "I'm sure you can find the way. Should you get lost, just ask one of the girls in my *harem* to show you."

I leave the room and do just that, stopping the first half-naked blond I see. With a skeptically raised eyebrow, she shows me through a labyrinthine set of corridors and into an elegant dining room overlooking the courtyard I'd only gotten glimpses of in the darkness before now. It's beautiful, and I hate that.

How men like Braulio and Jaguar love to cultivate their own personal collection of beautiful, delicate things. Even Diego had a few rose bushes that he treated with more care and delicacy than he ever showed me. I think that's the appeal for them—to show that they are capable of appreciating the quieter, lovelier side the world has to offer—and that they merely choose to sow misery and blood most of the time.

I find myself so enthralled watching the delicate blooms that I miss the moment I'm joined by their owner. His hand on my lower back is my only warning, and I jump at the contact. He grazed an open wound—on purpose, I suspect.

"I think I prefer this style to your usual, Tiena," he murmurs against the nape of my neck while fingering the sloppily cut edge of my makeshift ensemble. "Very sexy. But careful, chica. You might get an infection exposing such fresh wounds." He runs what feels like a thumb perilously close to the largest of the gruesome assortment. I have yet to inspect them in full, but judging from his low intake of air, the sight pleases him. "Though, you do look beautiful in red."

Why do I shiver when I hear that?

"I like to show off the various gifts I receive from powerful men," I tell him, still facing the garden view. "Not hide them."

"Sexy," he says with a chuckle, but his inflection dips toward that warning baritone. "I'd watch that angry magic tongue of yours, Lupe. Be careful you don't cut yourself on it."

"Why would I be angry?" I ask innocently.

He laughs again and hooks his hand beneath my chin to make me face him. His eyes sparkle with amusement, but they're narrowed in a way I don't like. This man is far more intelligent than he appears, missing nothing—not even a carefully concealed insult or a backhanded compliment.

Even Diego wasn't quite so perceptive.

"Because you don't like being played with like the little doll you are." He strokes my cheek as his upper lip quirks into the semblance of a grin. "I think you should ask my harem to give you tips in patience, chica. It is a virtue, after all."

I do a dangerous thing—I turn away from him and step closer to the window. He issues an ominous sound from the base of his throat, but when his hand fans across my back again, the touch is gentle. Thank God.

"Easy, Lupe. I've played nice until now, but let's be friends, *sí*? I don't think you want me as your enemy."

He's right. If Pedro were here, I know what he'd say—*Smile and shut the fuck up, Pita. You don't want to fuck with a man like him.* But maybe I do.

In retrospect, I can pinpoint the exact moment when things with Diego went too far. When he got the notion in his head that I would be more than a fling to him. That he would chase me to the ends of the earth and never let me escape his grasp.

It happened rather simply. One day, he captured my chin in a punishing grip and met my gaze directly. *What do you want from me, my sexy little butterfly?* he asked, his breath tinged with beer, his eyes bloodshot from whatever drug he'd snorted at the time. He'd been in a dangerous mental state, though I didn't know it then. The kind of mood where everything is taken literally, and he'd latch onto the smallest provocation.

Like a fool, I'd given him all the ammunition he'd needed to turn his full attention to me. *I only want you,* I told him. *I love you, Diego. I want to be with you forever.*

With those words, I'd signed my death certificate.

Since then, I've learned a valuable lesson—never give these men an inch more than you are willing to forfeit. To do so, is to lose everything.

"I think I would prefer to be your enemy than a part of your harem," I tell Jaguar. I mean every word, but he doesn't snarl in the face of them like I expect.

He merely nods. "Easy, Lupe. Let's not declare ourselves nemeses just yet. Come. Let's eat."

He retreats toward the center of the room, where a maid is in the middle of serving various platters of steaming food.

I consider spurning the request, but I note the way he's watching me. Keenly. I think he *wants* me to walk away. He wants me to fear being drugged again. He wants to lord his power over me without any resistance on my part.

So, I sit in the chair across from him instead, and set about making up a plate. To prove I'm not afraid, I sample a bit of an omelet and a few bites of fruit, all while struggling to ignore the pain shooting up and down my back.

He smiles and joins me, grabbing a slice of bacon. "I think we got off on the wrong foot," he tells me before taking a bite. As he licks his lips clean, he adds, "I'm willing to make things right, starting with my offer of getting you treatment for your back. You won't refuse."

There is more to the request than basic first-aid, but I have enough sense not to argue. I just nod. Pleased, he continues.

"And I even got you a present to make up for the misunderstanding. It will be here soon. *Claro?* In the meantime, I wish to show you more of my home should you let me."

He doesn't say it this time, but there is no choice in this instance, either. What could he possibly want to show me? My belly flips at the various possibilities.

"Eat up," he prods in response to my silence.

When I finally set my fork aside, he leans back in his chair and gestures around him. "You don't seem very impressed. Usually, when I bring women to my home, they have the sense to gush about the beauty. The luxury. They like to butter me up enough to then ask for a bit more money. Either you are used to far more extravagance or are way too modest for your own good. I'll give you a hint as to which theory I'm partial to—Braulio doesn't have a fraction of the money I do."

"Money isn't everything."

"Ah, your second lie, Tiena." He winks, wagging a disapproving finger at me. "You and I both know that money is everything. It is life or death. If I had none, you wouldn't be here right now, would you?"

"No," I say. "*Power* is everything—the money is merely secondary. Plenty of rich men have limited influence. I came to you for that. I wanted you to utilize that. Not parlor tricks or to placate me with luxury purses. I don't care about what I wear. I care about my son. I care about getting Braulio off our backs. I care about family."

"So, we have one thing in common then," Jaguar says softly. He shifts his stance, and I get the sense that he's shed part of the persona he was putting on for my benefit. I passed another test, though I'm not sure if I'm satisfied by the progress or annoyed. "Family is everything to me, Lupe. I go to war only for them. I don't let many into that category, either. How do I know that you would even be worth the risk?"

"I'm not," I say without caring how it sounds. There are some moral lines I refuse to cross, even at Pedro's behest. This is one. "I don't need family—I need a business partner."

Jaguar chuckles and takes a bite from a piece of toast. "Braulio did a number on you," he says, his tone still riding that lethally soft cadence. "You think I don't know the signs? A jumpy woman, eager to screw a stranger at the promise of assistance but hesitant to offer anything more. I think I would trust you more if you hated Braulio, but you still love him, don't you? That could make you a very dangerous friend, chica."

He couldn't be any more wrong. Still, I don't rush to refuse him just yet. The suspicion merely cements his belief that I am who he thinks I am. I don't think that's necessarily a bad thing.

"Love was never on the table between us," I point out.

Rather than take offense, he nods. "I think love from a woman as naughty as you would be a dangerous thing to covet indeed. Let's change the subject to something more palatable to us both. It's time for your present."

Dios mío, I can't smother a shudder of unease.

He claps his hands, and two men enter the room, dragging a third between them. That man sports a limp, and blood dribbles from his nose as he's allowed to fall to his knees near the head of the table. I have to pinch myself to keep the horror from my expression.

"Just in time," Jaguar says, pushing back in his seat. "Tiena, I would love for you to make introductions. I'm sure you recognize this man."

Panic shoots through me before I realize that I do, in fact, recognize him, though his face is swollen, his eyes bloodshot. Niles is his name. He did odd jobs for Braulio. I think he ran a minor ring in his distribution chain. It's only by sheer luck that I know as much. Tiena pointed him out to me, remarking how he always tried to stare up her skirt and reeked of weed.

His bloodshot eyes watch me warily, but there's a comical quality to the alarm that transforms his features. His lips twitch as his tanned skin turns several shades paler. Like he's seen a ghost. My heart pangs. He must think I'm Tiena. Is this further confirmation that she's dead?

Unfortunately, I can't ask him.

"Tiena?" Jaguar prods.

"He is Niles Rickman," I say, and he nods, pleased.

"Ah, yes. I'm sure you know what he does for your ex-lover—"

"Senior Domingas?" Niles struggles to speak around his swollen lip. "Mr. Braulio has no issue with you. He prizes your good relationship—"

"Exactly," Jaguar murmurs with a nod. "Then why has he been rushing to leave the country ever since my friend Ronaldo got a little too liberal with my books and drew my notice?"

Niles stammers an incoherent reply, but I feel my eyes widen.

Suddenly so many things click into place that it's overwhelming. Jaguar wasn't toying with me all this time. He was suspicious. Sending me to Ronaldo wasn't a ploy. It was a test, but not in the way I'd originally thought. He took my silence not as an abundance of caution but out of loyalty to Braulio. As his woman, I would know if he were the one paying Jaguar's accountants to turn him into the feds.

There is one flaw in that logic—Braulio isn't reckless. He's greedy. His motivation for going rogue had to go beyond simply wanting to upset the status quo.

Jaguar must be of the same frame of mind. No wonder he wanted to feed me to a pet panther. I meet his gaze, knowing he's watching my every reaction. *Finally*, he is giving me a taste of what I asked him for. A chance to prove my loyalty.

"That was very clever, finding the source of the discrepancies, chica," he praises, stroking his chin. "I must admit, I was skeptical when the whore of the bastard screwing me over comes begging me for help. Even you can't blame me for that. You should count your blessings, Tiena. That pretty little tongue has saved your life twice over. You handed me the information to ensure that Braulio has a very hard time leaving the country any time soon. I hope you're satisfied."

I'm not. I feel as though he kicked me in the stomach, and I regret eating anything. In a dizzying wave of nausea, it all threatens to come up as I relive the nightmare of Gatita's cage. God, I want to scream at him. Vomit in his face and dare him to punish me. I want…

For now, I want to live for Franco's sake.

Focus, Pita! Shaking my head to clear it, I hold his probing stare.

"I don't know what he does in his business," I admit in a rush. "But I told you the truth as I believe it to be. You are a powerful man. I avail myself only to powerful men."

And I can only imagine what might have happened to Francisco if Jaguar had burned Braulio's world to the ground and I hadn't been able to negotiate his safety in time. Would this man stoop to killing a child?

I'm sure he's done far, far worse.

Even his smile is violent. "Such sexy words you spin, chica," he says. "I hope you continue to be useful to me. You can start by joining me tonight. We'll have a lovely time, but I want to pick what you wear, beauty. *Claro?* Your current ensemble is a bit too edgy for my tastes."

I bristle at the extended timeline rather than the dig at my fashion choices. I'm already pushing it as it is if I want to be at the airport before my flight leaves. "I don't think someone like you would forget about my flight, Jaguar," I say.

A grunt of disapproval rumbles from his throat, making my heart skip a beat. "Oh no. You aren't going anywhere, *Tiena* —" His hands thud against the table, echoing like a gunshot. "Not until we get a few more details of our arrangement ironed out. Get this piece of shit out of here. I'll deal with him later."

The two men grab Niles and haul him from the room, but his eyes still dart to me, puzzled with confusion. It takes all the resolve I have to remain seated. What the hell does he know about Tiena?

I consider coming clean, and asking Jaguar to pump him for information—wherever he's taking Niles, I suspect it isn't to treat him to a meal and a tour of his home. One thing holds me back.

Francisco. As his supposed mother, I have a greater claim to him than as his aunt. Jaguar might be less willing to risk his life if the truth is revealed—and I'm all Franco has left if Tiena is dead. I can't let him stay in Braulio's hands, either.

Especially if the bastard has gotten himself into a bigger mess than I would have ever thought.

"You think Braulio is the one who paid off Ronaldo to steal from you," I say to Jaguar once his minions have left.

"'Paid off' makes it sound so harmless." He sits forward and steeples his hands together, propping his chin atop the point. "I think our friend Braulio is many things, chica, but stupid is not one of them. If he's making a move against me, he won't do so alone. Someone with far more balls than he has must be whispering in his ear. I'm sure you don't know who it could be?"

I shake my head. Rampant speculation isn't what he wants. Still, there is one suspicion I can't resist exploring.

"You thought I kept my silence about Ronaldo because I was in on the plan."

He chuckles without revealing an answer either way. "Those were very fancy calculations, chica. Capable of only someone who had a degree from some private ass college. But the methods he used? Oh, those were very specific. Braulio himself prefers those shell companies and fake LLCs. Almost as if whoever advised him in his own money dealings had tipped off straitlaced Ronaldo on how to get creative when hiding his theft from me. So, imagine my surprise when the woman rumored to handle Braulio's numbers shows up pledging her allegiance to me under a fake identity. Your saving grace is that even *he* isn't that sloppy."

Dear God. I suck in a breath as a chilling sense of relief washes over me. I came so close to a fate worse than being fed to a panther. No wonder Jaguar seems so amused by my actions.

From where he's sitting, they don't make any fucking sense.

"So, what changed your mind?" I manage to croak out, still rattled by his revelation.

"If you were truly guilty of trying to deceive me, you would have pleaded," he says, suddenly cold. "No one is that good of a liar, Lupe. You had the calm of a woman at peace with her truth. I can respect that."

"Enough to let me go to California as I planned?" I ask halfheartedly.

A lethal grin plays on his lips. "Enough to take you out for a night on the town and go from there," he says. "It's progress. Though, while I attend to some business around the house, I'd like for you to wait for me here. Can you do that? I assure you that you won't find a lack of entertainment."

I recognize another test, though I can't blame him. He'll have his men watch my every move, no doubt. He wants to see if I'll rush to tell Braulio about his supposedly missing friend. Should I refuse or try to leave, he'll jump to the worst-case scenario, and I'll have another up close and personal visit with Gatita.

Damn him. Damn him.

"What do you say, Tiena?" he asks.

"I've been dying to try out your pool," I say, my tone neutral.

He smiles. "I'm sure one of my girls can lend you a swimsuit, though you should take care with those wounds. Perhaps sunbathing would be safer."

"I'll swim, and I don't need a suit." I stand and head toward a pair of glass doors that lead to the terrace.

"Oh, and one more thing," Jaguar calls the exact second I think I'm safe from his scrutiny. "Maybe I was a bit hasty to introduce you to my kitty so soon, but you've recovered surprisingly well. Most women would be in shambles right now, begging for a sedative to take the bad memories away. You pretend to be rattled, I'll give you that, but you aren't in shock. That wasn't the first time you've seen men killed in front of you. Not shot or stabbed, but torn apart."

My steps falter. It takes me a second to recover from the shock, but I don't try to hide it. He's right.

But I won't let him drag out that secret anytime soon.

"Your pool looks divine," I simper, hurrying through the doors. Beyond them, I find a set of marble steps leading down to the pool, which thankfully is devoid of any other women.

Standing on the edge, I blind myself to everything but a need to separate myself from the rest of the world by any means possible. In the old days, that would mean inhaling, snorting, or smoking whatever scraps of his supply Diego sent my way to keep me compliant.

These days, pain is a better way to numb myself. I strip my altered dress, leaving on only my panties, and I dive in headfirst. Underwater, I let myself wince at the pain. It hurts so bad my mouth opens for a scream that's instantly smothered. When I resurface, however, I do so with a blank expression, and I push everything from my mind but a need to exist where nothing can touch me. Not Jaguar, not Diego or his memory.

Nothing.

The blissful peace doesn't last very long. A low, guttural laugh warns that my show has been viewed by someone who seems to have enjoyed it very much. His voice comes from nearby, perhaps at the doorway to the dining room.

"Enjoy it, chica," he calls out. "Make yourself at home. You've earned a reprieve. For now."

He's talking about more than answering his last question, though he never bothers to say so outright.

Only a foolish woman could ignore his meaning.

CHAPTER ELEVEN

I stay in the pool all damn day, and I don't leave it once. Not even to use the bathroom. I hold it instead, ignoring my straining bladder.

At some point, I roll onto my back and float, staring at the cloudless sky. On my millionth trip drifting around the pool, I notice a window above that must provide the view glimpsed from Jaguar's suite.

I stare directly into it and wonder if that's where he's chosen to conduct his business. He can see me, and I hope he takes comfort in the fact that I won't betray him.

And that most of his men lurk on the edges of the pool, watching me as well. I don't attempt to hide a damn thing, either. I let them stare, and I stretch my limbs leisurely, long after my fingers and toes have become wrinkled.

As the sun lowers on the horizon, I finally note a figure, clad in black, standing at the side of the pool, his arms crossed, smirk visible from here.

"I hate to interrupt your fun, Lupe," Jaguar says. He's fully dressed in a black silk shirt and jeans, his hair slicked back and glistening in the waning sunlight. "The night awaits. My friend here will help you get changed." He gestures to a beautiful, voluptuous blond who appears behind him.

I swim toward them and climb out, trying to hide my discomfort. I must have been in here for six hours at least, if not longer. As a result, my back is on fire, and I suspect that given the abundance of germs floating in this pool from the various women who play in it, I will probably get a nasty infection.

I'm not regretful, though. Thwarting Jaguar's latest mind game was well worth the risk, though I can't stifle a wince as I stand and accept the robe the woman hands me. It's short, made of pink silk, and reeks of perfume. I assume it belongs to one of the harem, but I tie it together over my front. From this angle, it's clear that an unusual number of men have positioned themselves in various spaces of the courtyard, averting their gaze as Jaguar places his hand on my lower back.

Possession radiates from his touch. It seems he is no longer in the mood to share me, at least. "Be quick," he warns, urging me toward the house.

I follow the woman inside and through a winding series of hallways. On the second floor, on the other side of the house from Jaguar's suite, is a large room with a four-poster bed, littered with stray bits of clothing.

"Is this your room?" I ask the woman.

"No. We usually just take our pick," the woman says quietly. "We don't own any of this. None of us do. But he requested you wear this…" She guides me into the closet and fishes a red dress from a hanger.

It's gorgeous but far more risqué than anything Pedro would suggest I wear. In essence, it's merely a long strip of scarlet silk designed to wrap around my neck to cover my breasts and ties around my waist to form a barely-there skirt.

The woman then shows me into a large bathroom and uses a blow-dryer on my hair to make it stick straight before applying heavy makeup.

The result is that I look nothing like myself. I resemble the caricature of Tiena that Braulio would parade around. She dressed like this. Did her makeup like this. Jaguar, it seems, has done his homework.

"You're to see the doctor next," the blond says. She leads me downstairs and into what looks like a makeshift clinic. There is a row of counters, an industrial-style sink, and an examination table.

There a woman gives me a once over. She's beautiful in her own right, at least in her mid-forties, with her blond hair in a loose bun and a white lab coat draped over her modest sweater and jeans. She could be the usual clinician I've dealt with all my life if it weren't for the fact that she's washing her hands in a sink splattered with what looks like fresh blood. Drying on a countertop nearby is an array of knives and sharp instruments that don't seem like the usual doctor's toolkit.

Were they used on Niles, perhaps? It seems Jaguar doesn't feed all his enemies to his kitty.

Spotting me, the woman sighs and dries her hands on a towel. "Come in. He wants you on birth control if you aren't already," she says without even introducing herself. As suspected, my back was the least of Jaguar's concerns.

"I have an implant," I tell the woman, raising my arm.

She frowns and looks across the room toward a desk piled with various documents. "Interesting. That wasn't in your medical file."

Tiena's medical file, because, of course, Jaguar managed to procure it. Curiosity itches. I wonder about all the medical procedures she hid from me. Any scars she obscured that would betray in a heartbeat I'm not really her.

Like her *laissez-faire* attitude when it came to contraception. Franco was only one of four pregnancies I know of. He just happened to be conceived when she was desperate to secure Braulio's affections—the most powerful man she'd snagged by that point. I knew she wasn't eager to have more children with him, but if she could move onto a man like Jaguar? She'd get pregnant in a heartbeat. The thought chills me to the core.

"I learned that a smart woman has her secrets," I say to the doctor, who is still watching me, waiting for a response.

She scoffs. "Not anymore, you don't. Write down what you remember, and I'll verify the dosage. Jaguar prefers oral contraceptives that I can monitor, but this should suffice. Now lie down on your stomach so I can treat those wounds. You're courting danger, leaving them exposed like that. The narcos are vicious, but so is a blood infection. I've seen Gatita's handiwork turn nasty before. Only God knows what kind of microbes are on that animal's claws."

After making me swallow a pill she claimed was an antibiotic, she cleans my wounds, but opts to leave them uncovered. I suspect the choice wasn't hers, but Jaguar's. He wants to display his twisted masterpiece.

As I redress, I sense the doctor come up behind me, her breath hot on my neck. Assuming she wants to inspect my wounds, I don't react. Not until she snatches my wrist in a punishing grip. "Who are you?"

Alarm prickles my spine at the hostility in her tone. "T-Tiena Sanchez," I say, turning to face her.

"No. You aren't." She steps back, her gaze cold. "I may not be well versed in the crime syndicate, but I know my way around a human body. You may look like the woman he says you are, but according to her file, she had a C-section six years ago. No plastic surgeon is good enough to hide that kind of scarring."

Shit. I hate that cliché line—*I saw my life flash before my eyes.* When Diego beat me within an inch of my life, I never saw anything but blood and darkness. No charming memories. No glimpse of what might have been.

But for the first time, I understand that phrase intimately. I see a fleeting snippet of the future I could have had with

Francisco. Then, I see the horror awaiting me in Gatita's cage, once again at Jaguar's mercy.

Not that I'll submit to him weakly this time. Hell no. I won't go down without a fight.

"Easy," the doctor says with a shrug. "I don't give a fuck what your name is. What I do care about, however, is that I can do my job. Get me your real file. Do that, and you can call yourself the queen of England as long as I know exactly who I'm dealing with. I won't have an issue with a medication error because some bitch wants to stay under the radar. Jaguar knows that I'm not his game warden."

Something in her tone makes me suspect that this isn't the first time she's dealt with women hiding their true identities. Though, I'm sure that plenty of frightened souls hop from narco to narco, desperate for a safe place to stay.

"I will," I say hoarsely.

"Good." She brushes me off with a dismissive wave. "Now run along."

As I leave her makeshift clinic, a harem beauty doesn't appear to show me the way. I wander aimlessly, afraid that I might accidentally stumble upon Gatita's cage.

Near a set of stairs that hopefully lead to the front of the house, a sudden noise makes me stop short. This section of the hall is empty, but there's a room nearby with the door slightly ajar. I inch toward it, and another muffled noise is my reward. A whimper?

A swatch of pitch-black darkness is all I can make out through the cracked doorway, but when a masculine voice rings out, I think I recognize it.

"...the bitch. She set him up," a man moans. Niles?

The sharp, accented voice that answers him is easier to peg —Horatio. "Who? I need a name."

A high-pitched whine echoes off the walls, and I inch backward, my heart in my throat. Only God knows what kind of torture could make such a sound. Something far worse than even Gatita's claws.

"That bitch," Niles repeats frantically. "That cunt Tiena—"

"Hey!"

I jump and whirl around to find a blond woman gazing down at me from the top of the stairs. With a curt nod, she beckons me toward her, and seconds later, I'm shown into the foyer and unceremoniously reunited with Jaguar. He smiles at my appearance, but despite his insistence of the contrary, he doesn't seem more impressed with this version of me than the prior iterations.

"Beautiful," he says, regardless. When I come close enough, he takes my hand and brings my fingers to his lips. The gesture doesn't feel charming in the slightest. It's a warning. All I can hear is Nile's voice naming Tiena as an accomplice. To Ronaldo's scheme or something worse?

In any case, it's not like I can ask him.

Smiling, he releases me and heads for the door. "Shall we?"

This time, we take a red sports car but are followed by what seems like his full entourage. At least ten men and women pile into several vehicles and tail us to a high-rise in the heart of the city.

"Tonight, one of my lieutenants is having a little party," Jaguar explains, to my utter alarm. Visually, he seems casual enough, leaning back with one hand on the steering wheel, but I'm not fooled. He isn't the type to dole out exposition for the hell of it. "We shouldn't be long. We're here merely to mingle."

"You don't strike me as the mingling type," I say, risking his ire.

To my surprise, he smiles in that charming way, but it doesn't reach his eyes. "You'll see."

When we finally exit the car, Jaguar leads me inside on his arm while four women from his harem flank us on either side. I'm tense the entire trip through a spacious lobby and into a glass elevator leading up.

The second we arrive on the rooftop floor, I realize exactly why he brought me here. While I rarely accompanied Tiena to her social gatherings, I recognize a narco party when I see it. The excess of wealth and the opulent glamor are unmistakable—nothing at all like the small get-together he made it seem. Not to mention, every man here looks far too dangerous to be mingling around a buffet for the hell of it.

I can only think of a few chilling explanations for our visit here. One, he wanted to show me off—but not out of vanity.

Those in the nearest vicinity to us turn our way and audibly gasp at the sight of me. Tiena in the flesh. These aren't any old party guests, either. They're all friends of Braulio. I recognize their faces from years spent in Tiena's periphery, though I know none personally.

They, however, seem to take Jaguar's stylistic choices at face value. I'm *her*, fresh from exile.

And where his friends linger, I'm sure Braulio himself isn't far behind.

Damn.

Damn.

Damn.

"You seem nervous, Tiena," Jaguar murmurs against my ear as we step out of the posh elevator that brought us to this open-air level. "Don't tell me you're feeling shy."

I am. None of these strangers know the truth, but there is one tiny flaw in my plan that I haven't let myself consider—Braulio does. He knows about my existence, and if Tiena really is dead, he'll know instantly that I'm not her. He'll have no reason to keep his mouth shut either, and there goes my ruse.

Dios mío, I can't let him see me.

"I need to use the restroom," I whisper, inching toward the thickest press of people.

"Oh no, you don't." Jaguar grabs my hand, gripping it tight. A hard tug on his part yanks me into him, and I'm effectively trapped. "You're going to stay by my side, and we'll see how good of an actor dear Braulio is. One more test, chica. Let's hope you pass, huh? I've grown accustomed to that sexy little ass."

He pinches the ass in question while I scan the room wildly for Braulio. I don't see him—yet.

He'll arrive sooner or later. It's only a matter of seconds. *Run, Pita.*

My captor, however, doesn't seem inclined to let me go.

"We should dance," Jaguar murmurs, his glee apparent. "I wonder how well you can make that body move off my cock."

His tone triggers an irritation I can't bite back.

"You've offered me up as bait, Jaguar," I say, fighting to keep my voice under control. I don't look at him, instead keeping my focus on the crowd and any passerby who could potentially be Braulio.

"Ah, don't sound so angry, chica." Jaguar strokes my cheek with his thumb. "You are beautiful, tempting bait. After all, if you left that bastard of your own accord, you don't need to fear him when you're around me. Unless you've been *lying*, Tiena. In that case, Braulio is the least of your worries."

I don't shiver in face of the threat. Maybe it's a blessing in disguise.

"I have been lying," I admit, my voice breaking. It's risky to come clean now, but it's better to do so before anyone else can ruin the surprise for me. With my gaze still darting from partygoer to partygoer, I decide it's well worth the risk. "Braulio will be very surprised to see me, because I'm not—"

"It seems you spoke too soon," Jaguar growls, inclining his head in the opposite direction. "And he seems very, very surprised to see you, chica."

"W-What?"

Heart heavy with dread, I turn in the direction Jaguar indicates and tremble. Braulio himself stands paces away, his eyes on my face. He's dressed in his typical gaudy attire —a white tank top adorned with countless gold chains, and his shaved head on display. His expression, however, catches me off guard, and I fight to school mine into a blank mask. He doesn't look angry to see me, or even shocked. His eyes go wide instead, and his usual shit-eating grin is absent. Much like Niles, he looks as though he's seeing a ghost.

For a second, concern for my sister worms to the forefront of my mind. Tiena… *What the hell have you gotten yourself into?* If she were afraid that Braulio could put his own son in the hospital with little provocation, what in the world was he capable of doing to her?

"Talk to him," Jaguar commands, shoving me forward. "Make sure you brag about how good of a girl you've been for me."

I stagger on my borrowed heels and try to think. *Focus, Pita!*

Braulio makes no move to approach me first, and I consider running. It would be better to do so than be unmasked here in the open. Before I can wrestle my body into submission, I sense movement behind me.

"Braulio, come," Jaguar calls, robbing me of the chance to flee. "Say hello to my friend. I've been told you two were acquainted."

"Jaguar." Braulio finally advances, but his expression doesn't switch to smug confidence. As he draws even with me, he rams his shoulder against mine. "You little cunt," he murmurs too softly for Jaguar to hear. "You lying bitch—"

"Come." A familiar grip seizes my hand and pulls me back against a broad shoulder and a body carved from solid muscle. "She's beautiful, isn't she? What did you say your name was, baby? Lupita?" Jaguar asks. He speaks loudly enough for Braulio to hear, and at the sound of my name, his eyes widen. He can't help himself.

With fresh curiosity, he flicks his gaze toward me again, but triumphant isn't what I'd call his expression. It's utter fear, and I can guess the source. *Tiena.* Whatever she's gotten herself into, he thinks I'm in on it.

"It's good to see you, Jaguar," he says, having gotten himself under control. His gruff voice makes my skin crawl, and I bite my lip to avoid demanding answers about Franco. "You know I am always open to meeting with you, but I have prior engagements. If you'll excuse me." He gestures to the two men who lurk in his shadow—a drastic difference from his usual crew of hangers-on. It's not the number that alarms me, but the fact that they both carry themselves with unmistakable alertness—these men are bodyguards, not Braulio's usual sycophants. He's come prepared tonight.

For what?

Teeth bared in a feral smile, Jaguar doesn't offer up any hint as to what he might be planning. "Ah, and Braulio?" he adds before the man can fade into the crowd. "If you see Niles, send him my way. I wanted to discuss an issue with his route."

Braulio inclines his head, seemingly unaware of the grisly fate of his trusted ally. "*Sí.*"

As he leaves, Jaguar retreats from me, releasing my arm. I stiffen, picking up on a sudden change—his entire mood has shifted. Something's wrong. No longer is he smug or confident or even angry. Whatever he expected from this little stunt, he didn't seem to get.

But why?

And Braulio... He didn't rush to expose me as an imposter of Tiena. Instead, he seemed... Afraid. I've seen the same man order my sister around like a tyrant and threaten grown men without batting an eyelash. Never have I seen him cower before—and never has he looked at me like that. Like he thought I was playing some horrific role in a game against him. One he was only now starting to grasp.

Ice runs down my spine, triggering a wave of nausea. What the hell has Tiena done?

Something bad. Perhaps Braulio isn't alone in his sudden need for a bodyguard. I feel exposed out in the open under my assumed identity—and it seems Jaguar has changed his mind about extending his protection. He's left me gaping on the threshold of the party, and I spy him halfway across the rooftop with his harem of minions. When I attempt to follow him, I'm jostled by those nearby who seem eager to get my attention.

"Tiena," someone murmurs, grabbing for my arm. "Where in the hell have you been, girl?"

Another hand brushes my shoulder, but I evade the touch and flee. Turning on my heel, I retreat to the periphery of the rooftop, desperate for air. God, what to do? I should leave. Try to reschedule my flight and forsake this stupid plan.

I even take a step toward the elevator we came in through.

Only one thing makes me hesitate—I think of Franco. Of his beautiful face and the way his hazel eyes had seemed hollow beside the bruise I saw on him last. There is no way in hell I can leave him to the whims of that monster with no way out. I can't...

"You stupid bitch."

A hard surface presses into my lower back, heedless of the wounds there. I hiss through my teeth, but a hand clamps over my mouth, smothering any cry I make. In the same instance, someone steps in front of me, blocking my body from view of anyone in nearby proximity.

"You dumb, twisted little cunt," my captor growls. "I knew Tiena was a sick little bitch, but you, Lupe? What the fuck did she tell you, huh? If you think she has your back, you're wrong. She's already sold you out, you stupid bitch. We're both dead—"

Braulio. I recognize his voice, which means he must be the owner of the unseen weapon digging into my skin. I should be afraid, I think. Deep down, a part of me knows that. As the seconds tick past, I don't feel a damn thing.

Just irritation. Emboldened by it, I bite down on his hand until he wrenches it free, gripping my throat instead. "I don't know, Braulio," I choke out. "Why don't you ask her? Where is she—"

"Shut the fuck up." He shoves the object into me hard, and I wince. Fire sears through the deepest wound, and a warm substance drips down my hip a heartbeat later.

"I should have known better than trust her stupid ass plan. That little cunt shoots her mouth off, and then some sick motherfucker comes asking about *you*. Did you set me up from the fucking start?"

Asking about me? "Jaguar? You were a fool to move against him in the first place. Did you even think about what could happen to Franco?"

"Don't play dumb, Lupita. Did you think about what could happen to you? Tiena isn't here to protect you, not that she fucking would." Laughing, Braulio maneuvers me away from the main party to a vacant corner filled only with crates of electronic equipment.

"I knew that cunt was planning something stupid, but this takes the cake," he says, sounding borderline incoherent. His grip tightens to a painful degree, drawing a hiss from my lips that I can't smother. "I played along, let her use me like a fucking puppet—but I'm not as dumb as you bitches think. She thought she could make an outside deal? Well, so did I. Fuck her. When you see her in Hell, tell that bitch I said hello."

"So you killed her, then." I don't anticipate the pain I feel. Despite everything she's done, I'll always love her, no matter the cost to me.

But Braulio doesn't rush to gloat. He keeps rambling. "She set me up. Told me to hire that fucking accountant. Then, to cover her bases, she sent you after Jaguar the second shit got too hot. God damn her." He sounds hysterical. Incoherent almost, and that weapon bites into me deeper and deeper. It's a gun. I recognize the shape, and my heart begins to beat a little faster. At the rate he's going, he might miss a clean kill and make it hurt. "But tell me, where does he come into play? That other fucker? The one with the eye patch? When he first asked about you, I thought he was being slick. You don't mean shit to anyone. But he wanted you so badly, you little cunt. Damn near threatened to cut my balls off if I didn't do what he wanted, but no one puts the screws to me. No fucking one—"

"Jaguar?" I ask again. My heart lurches as a tiny voice in my head whispers, *Oh, you poor thing. You know it wasn't him...*

"I don't remember the fucker's name," Braulio hisses. "He talked a big ass game, but he knew the plan. I'm sure you bitches roped him in. Oh, you stupid cunt. I knew you were psychotic, but stupid? You must be if you and that bitch sold me out. The joke's on you. I'm the one in control now, and you? You're already dead—"

"Apparently, Tiena's dead, too," I snap. "So, what next? You kill me here and run off with your tail between your legs?"

"Kill you? Oh no, Pita. That's not the deal I made. He asked for you alive, that sick fuck. You must have crossed him real bad. But why should I? He can have your body for all I fucking care."

He shoves me forward, and I realize we're approaching a battered metal door that must lead to a staircase. *No*, a part of me warns. If I let him take me, I'll be as good as dead.

I dig my heels into the floor, and try to distract him. *Think, Pita!*

"Who asked about me?" I ask, straining my neck to meet his gaze from over my shoulder. Stalling him is only partly behind my curiosity. Apart from Jaguar, I don't know who could want me. Did Tiena rope another narco into her scheme?

"I remember now, his name." Without warning, he shoves me down and slams his foot into my back.

It hurts. I can't silence a scream, though a laugh edges it. I didn't think Braulio had it in him to hit someone who wasn't cowering in response. Like Tiena. Like his son. He's gotten bolder since I saw him last.

"Whatever Tiena did to you, you deserved it," I tell him, rolling onto my stomach. At the same time, I scan the nearest stack of crates for anything I can use as a weapon. God, I can't let him take me. "Do you hear me, you stupid bastard? You deserve it!"

"And you deserve what's waiting for you, too, Lupita. He told me what he has in mind for you, and it is sick shit. Ah, now I remember. His name," Braulio says as though I never spoke. He kicks me again, so hard I wheeze. Then he levels his pistol at my skull. "Diego—"

"Leave the woman and go," a voice commands. I vaguely recognize it. Dazed, I look up and see a lanky figure standing paces away. I know him. The man from last night. Horatio. "Now. Before Jaguar decides to make it clear that his woman is not to be touched. Go."

Footsteps echo wildly, and I assume Braulio retreats, but my vision is too blurry to see by. I just lie here, tasting blood on my tongue and feeling it drip down my back.

"Come, miss." Horatio hooks a hand beneath my waist and hauls me to my feet. He brings me into the elevator and then through a darkened lobby. There must be a car waiting nearby. I'm shoved onto a spacious back seat, but when a familiar voice trickles into my ear, I realize I'm late for the party.

"Bad luck, chica," Jaguar says with a sigh. "Braulio can be very possessive. I should have known better than to parade you before him. Horatio told me he had a gun to your skull, but you were still running your mouth, cursing him to hell and back. Sexy."

I say nothing, turning my face into the seat cushions instead. Various aches and pains make themselves known all over my body, but they are nothing compared to the minefield that is my mind.

Braulio was lying, of course. I misheard him. I let my old friend fear sneak up on me and distort reality. There is no way I heard that name. No way.

"If you were my woman, I would have put him in his place, but you aren't, are you? You still belong to him."

Anger laces his tone though I don't have the space of mind to wonder why.

"What? No spicy comeback?" I hear Jaguar say, but he might as well be on another planet. Few things can penetrate the hellscape of my consciousness. Not until I regain my control.

I had to have misheard him.

I was delirious.

He lied—Tiena gave him ammunition to use against me, because we are all just pawns in one of her schemes. She set up that trick with the accountant. She's working with a powerful enemy against Jaguar, but who?

Not him. He can't be back. It isn't possible. It's been ten years. Ten years… Besides, I saw him die.

I pulled the trigger—and Lupita Sanchez had to die along with him.

It feels like only a handful of seconds have passed when the car stops again, and I'm hauled out by someone who must be Horatio. He keeps his touch clinical but firm—his strength is the only thing holding me up.

It's foolish to show weakness here in a den of lions, but even Jaguar and his posse don't compare to the real Boogeyman haunting my nightmares. Last night was one of the first times he managed to assert himself in my memories, but this time it's so much more intense. I hear him.

Oh, Pita baby, you thought I'd just quietly disappear? That I would ever let you go? We're soul mates, butterfly. You will always be mine. Always. Till death do us part.

"Enough, chica." Jaguar's voice penetrates my battered psyche only because he sounds so different from his usual smug cadence. His voice is harsher, lacking the suave charm. Impatient. I get the sense he's spoken to me many, many times since we left the car, but I haven't heard a damn thing.

"I've enjoyed your little display, but you can drop the act, Tiena. I know Braulio doesn't scare you half as bad as I should."

But Braulio isn't the real threat.

"Eyes on me," Jaguar warns, snapping his fingers inches from my nose.

I look up, surprised to find that we're in his suite. He crosses to the window and leans against it, a shot of whiskey in hand, but his smirk is gone, replaced by a cold, hard stare. This, I suspect, is the real Julian Domingas beneath the raucous, brutal façade.

I misjudged him by slotting him into the same category as Braulio and the other men I'd dealt with. He is a new animal entirely, one I'd underestimated until now. Unlike them, emotions don't guide him. The bastard is one-hundred percent pure calculation like a robot, reacting to the world on probability and educated guesses. He isn't reactionary.

He is far more intelligent than that.

"You put on a good show," he tells me. "I'm impressed. Few women have made me rethink my first impression like you have. I'm sorry to say, your show has run its course, though. I see who you are now, Tiena."

"You put on a good show, too," I tell him coldly, swaying on trembling legs. Fear isn't the cause. I'm so damn exhausted. "Have you enjoyed toying with me from the start? I hope you got a nice, big kick out of it. Plenty of fuel when you fuck your harem, or are they only for show? Do you just use them as toys in your display?"

"Oh, chica, I don't know what you mean." Smiling, he takes a sip of his liquor, but the amusement never reaches his eyes. "Do tell."

"I was fooled at first," I admit. God, why does my voice sound so breathless? So broken? If he's dropped his act, then so have I. I'm not Tiena, primed to charm my way out of every situation by smiling and flashing my tits. I've always been far more pathetic, prone to the two emotions she never let stand in her way.

Love and fear.

"I'm sure you have the world convinced you're all brute action. A mindless idiot who uses his minions to inspire fear. Oh, you have them all fooled, Jaguar. But you've met your match in me."

"Is that so?" He laughs, but it's a dangerous mixture of guttural rumbles. "Please continue, Tiena. I find this all very fascinating."

"I know brutes. I was infected with one once. I know how they operate and move, and there is no calculation involved."

The memories threaten to overwhelm me—dark, horrific things. It's getting harder than ever to keep them at bay, but I don't need much to make a definitive conclusion where he is concerned.

"You are patient, Jaguar. Too patient. You don't thrive on inspiring fear. You don't play with your victims like toys in a game. They're pawns to you. Tools. You don't give a fuck about women, or power, or damn assholes like Braulio. It's the thrill of staying one step ahead that you crave. You think we're all too dumb to see how pointless you find this."

"And how have I played with you, Tiena?" He sets his shot glass down hard enough that liquid spills over the rim. "Perhaps, you should explain how you sought to play with *me*? Strolling into my orbit as if I wouldn't fucking recognize you as Braulio's bitch. Aiming to fuck your way into my good graces. Concealing that you were in on that motherfucker's little scheme from the start. Oh, please do enlighten me. Were you surprised I'm not the dumb motherfucker you seemed to think I am?"

"Yes," I admit, my voice rasping. "I prefer men who act like animals. At least there is no coherent reason behind the abuse they inflict. Survival is their aim, not boredom. They know when to stop once their prey is already dead."

God, do I know that firsthand. I'm crying. Tears spill down my face, and I hadn't even realized. Only he can do this to me—a beast that conditioned me to live my entire life relying on fear. Avoiding the nuances in his moods that shifted like the wind. Jaguar is far more dangerous, but he doesn't frighten me half as much as even the mere memory of Diego does.

Jaguar has used my body as his plaything, but Diego? He got inside my head. Inside my very soul. My entire being was his toy. It still is.

"Just tell me now." I can't look at Jaguar any longer, turning my gaze to the floor. "You've been working with him all this time. It's why you used the cage. It's why you…"

I was so stupid not to see the parallels before. So stupid.

"Where is he?" I ask, but my voice breaks into a hysterical bubble of laughter. Of course, he won't step from the shadows on cue like some TV villain. Diego was always far more nuanced than that. When he would disappear on me for days at a time, he would only resurface when provoked.

When I broke one of his rules for even a second. When I dared to hope he'd grown tired of me for good.

I know what will draw him out now.

I spy the view of the pool through partially-opened glass doors. A balcony extends over it, and I'm sure his entire posse is gathered around to watch this display. Jaguar will bluff about killing me tonight, but he won't. That's why I've made it this long in one piece.

Diego always gets his prize in the end. Always.

"I don't think our conversation is over, Lupe," I hear Jaguar growl.

I ignore him.

Running gives me a fast enough start to race through the terrace doors and vault over the railing without slowing. The speed propels me over the barrier, and then it's a terrifying freefall.

These moments used to be the only times I found comfort. When I had the faintest hope of finally, finally ending my torment in the one way Diego couldn't circumvent. He always did in the end, though. Even death wasn't strong enough to keep me from him.

Sooner or later, reality—like gravity—would kick in.

Wham! I hit resistance so hard that the air is knocked from my lungs. Stars dance across my vision, and then everything goes black…

For a heartbeat.

The next, I'm weightless, surrounded by blissful, freezing darkness. I linger for as long as I can stand it. Resurfacing feels like an unsurmountable chore, and I consider never doing so. Staying down here until my lungs explode. Letting death finally take me once and for all.

As if it would be so easy.

When my lungs scream for air too badly to ignore, I kick toward the surface of the pool and gulp for breath. With my eyes burning and blurry, I hunt for him. He should appear now as he always did, pleased by my display. I played his favorite game, and he doesn't disappoint.

Then it happens. Clapping slowly, he appears at the edge of the pool, but wait…

He's too tall, too bulky. Those eyes aren't right either, a dark, haunting brown instead of green.

"A beautiful display, chica," Jaguar says in a tone too cold to be praise. "If you were aiming to kill yourself, it seems you missed—"

"No." I don't recognize the voice that rings out, or perhaps I don't want to. It belongs to a nightmare of a woman I've spent the past decade trying to forget. The creature Diego made of me, his Pita. "I want him. Where is he? Where is he? I know he's here, right? He has to be. Tell him I'm ready for him. So where is he?"

I glance around the pool, waiting for Diego. His smile. That knowing tilt to his head when I've done something he likes. That low, unsettling rasp of his voice.

Diego.

Diego…

"Braulio isn't here, chica. I hate to disappoint you."

"Stop lying to me! I was stupid enough to think that you were different than them, but you're not, are you? You have no honor. You're a pig like the rest—"

"Your spicy tongue, I don't mind. But insults? Oh no, Lupe. That I won't tolerate." Jaguar sheds his shirt and jumps into the pool before I can react. With a swift few strokes, he's before me.

"Give me one more thing," he says softly, treading water just beyond my reach. "One more question I want you to answer before I finally decide whether or not to trust you."

"I don't care if you trust me," I spit. "Your help means nothing anymore!"

If Diego is out there, Franco is better anywhere than with me. Even with Braulio. I'll have to find a way to wire him money. Get him somewhere safe with people who can take care of a six-year-old child.

Whatever it takes, I have to try.

"Did you hear me?" Jaguar runs his thumb along my mouth, forcing me to meet his gaze. "I will admit that you never cease to amaze me, Tiena. Braulio was supposed to threaten you. Rough you up, perhaps. But kill you? I didn't think the bastard had it in him to go that far. He likes his women on leashes, under his control. He doesn't have the balls for murder. You must have one hell of a secret in that skull, chica. Whatever it is, it's now mine."

"And I'll never tell you a damn thing. Never," I add, emboldened by agony and adrenaline. "Not everyone can be manipulated by fear."

"Ah, you will be. Or you forfeit that precious son of yours. A good mother wouldn't do that, would she?"

Fear shoots down my spine, but I don't allow it to distract me. "I'm of better use to him dead than alive," I say, meaning every word. "And I'm not afraid to die, Jaguar. I'm sure *he* told you that, didn't he? Threaten me all you want. I don't fear pain. I fear…"

Him. *Diego.* Only now can I admit that.

"I don't know what deal you made with him, but it will backfire. You think he's let you have me, but he hasn't," I say, tripping over my words. God, I can't stop looking for him, craning my neck to see beyond Jaguar. Only his posse is in view, though. "He will always own me. You will only ever have pieces. Just scraps. Never the whole thing."

Even I don't have that luxury. For the first time in a decade, I feel like I have no control of my own limbs. I'm just a creature composed of fear and pain, eager to escape her next dose of both.

"Oh no, you don't." Jaguar grips my arm the second I try to move and wrenches me toward him. "Come here—"

I lunge away though I know escape is futile. I'm not fast enough. I'm not strong enough. Nevertheless, I am skilled enough in the ways of violent men to know exactly when to let go. When to allow his full force to pull me along without resistance.

I practically sail through the water in the direction of the ledge. And when my head strikes off the firm surface, I know that, before everything goes black…

I'm smiling.

CHAPTER TWELVE

Everything hurts, but if the pain was all I had to contend with, I'd be a happy woman. After all, agony and I are old friends.

This sensation, however, is new. Someone bandaged me while I was out. They drugged me too, but not with the harsh, sharp substances I grew accustomed to all those years ago. The feeling is softer, more soothing than stimulating—a mild analgesic and perhaps something else so that I don't feel as shaky as I should.

Whoever my nursemaid was, they dressed me, too—in a stiff, cotton button-up that feels several sizes too big.

The inside of my mouth tastes like cotton, and the air… It smells like cheap perfume, nail polish, and sweat.

"Tiena?" I hear myself rasp. She's the only person in the world I know of who reliably smells like all three. How fitting would it be for her to turn up now?

"You're awake." The voice is haughty like hers, but too high-pitched.

When I peel my eyes open, the blurry figure I find perched nearby is not my sister. She's too pale, and her hair is far too bright. As my vision comes into clearer focus, I realize she's a beautiful carbon copy of the rest of the girls in Jaguar's harem.

She wears a tiny bikini top paired with white shorts and sits with her back to me on the edge of what seems to be a large bed. Her large blue eyes flick over me in disapproval, and with a sigh, she stands and runs a manicured hand through her blond hair.

"He wants you in his suite. Follow me."

She heads for the doorway, but I don't move. Jaguar can wait. No longer am I in the mood to jump for his approval.

"You are one dumb, crazy, psycho bitch. He'll make you regret this," the woman remarks before flouncing away.

Unconcerned, I roll over to put my back to the door and focus on taking in the rest of the room. It resembles the one I got dressed in what seems like a lifetime ago. I wonder how many spare bedrooms he has, rented out to the various floozies he utilizes to keep up appearances. The man is smart. He uses his harem not only to fuel a healthy appetite for sex, but for a more important purpose—anonymity. It makes him seem aloof and unwilling to attach himself to one key woman. As Braulio is finding out, when the world knows the main woman you stick your cock into, you have a key weakness for anyone to exploit.

Diego made the same mistake, but he did not fear me, as Braulio sometimes seemed intimidated by Tiena. No. I would rather die than betray him, so no one could ever use me against him. Love he called it. I think a better phrasing was a complete and total corruption of my soul.

Despite the depth of his ownership, he isn't here now to claim me. I feel his absence in my bones the way I could always sense his nearness back then. If Jaguar did have him lurking out of sight somewhere, he's gone. I guess my display wasn't good enough.

Though it seems to have gotten the notice of someone. Heavy footsteps still near the door of this room, and a voice rings out, "That was a very dangerous stunt you pulled, Lupe." It's Jaguar's. Lurking within the low notes is the first sign of real anger in him I think I've sensed. Those glimpses of it before were nothing. Mirages. His real fury is as potent as a wildfire and just as reckless. "I knew you were spicy, but foolish? That I did not have on my bingo card."

"And I didn't know you were this sadistic," I rasp without lifting my head. "You and he have plenty in common. I'm sure you bonded over that."

It's pathetic. I can't even say his name.

"Again, with Braulio." Jaguar makes a low sound in his throat, too guttural to be laughter. "You might be pleased to know that he went into hiding after that display last night —but I think you have me mistaken, chica. You were the one conspiring with that *pendejo* against me. I would appreciate it if you would come clean."

He means it, and I realize how much of an idiot I've been, letting him wind me up like a toy and watch me go.

No more.

"If I were working with Braulio, I wouldn't be stupid enough to fool you. I'd leave the damn country. A plan as reckless as playing with your accountant was doomed to fail. Only a fucking idiot would think otherwise."

And perhaps that was exactly what Tiena has done if she's still alive. Flee. Leave behind her own son because she couldn't risk being tracked by anyone. Not even me.

"An idiot, *or* a clever little whore. You thought that sexy mouth could fool me," Jaguar says when I fall silent. "You thought I was a stupid, mindless fucker like the many assholes you've screwed. Didn't you?"

The bed dips alarmingly, and I picture him climbing onto it, reaching for me. His palm slips beneath my borrowed shirt to strike my bare ass, but nowhere near hard enough to hurt. He grips the globe of it instead, his hand's calloused, rippling with lethal tension.

"Come clean, chica. I'm sure you can make it up to me." His voice drips into my ear, his breath on my cheek. "What was it you said last night? I'll only ever have pieces of you. Funny. The first night you came to me, you told me I could have all of you. Was that never in Braulio's grand plan?"

"I'm tired, Jaguar." Truly, I am. Clearly too tired to play the role of frightened captive he seems to crave. "Just call him back and drop the charade."

I'm not talking about Braulio.

"I'm surprised he let you keep me this long," I add. Sharing was never Diego's forte.

Almost a decade freed from his influence, yet I clearly remember what it was like under his spell. The role to take on. The right words to say. How to cower. My body employs those tactics now against Jaguar purely out of habit. I hunch away from him and tense against his touch.

And he takes offense to that. His scoff alone conveys that, at least in this instance, he isn't fucking around. Neither Braulio nor Diego is here. Odd.

"It seems we've gotten off on the wrong foot again," he says. "Look at me."

The bed shifts again, and his hand latches onto my wrist, hauling me upright. It hurts. My head is on fire, my back a searing inferno of agony. He makes me face him, anyway, perched on the end of the bed while he crouches on one knee. Already resting at his feet is a partially opened first-aid kit. Was the blond I saw earlier the one who bandaged me?

Without revealing as much, Jaguar fishes a clean rag from the case and reaches for my chin.

"Let's start over, shall we?" He dabs at my forehead, and I can't silence a wince. It's the source of the pain radiating throughout the rest of my skull. "I am Julian Domingas, and you are?"

I don't answer him, eyeing his face instead. His eyes betray the anger his voice conceals. They're burning like coals, radiating energy that jolts through me.

"Answer me, chica," he warns, still dabbing at my throbbing forehead. "And you are?"

"Skeptical, Jaguar," I say.

"Still so feisty. Lift your chin." He dabs at my neck next with surprisingly gentle motions. I'm not fooled. "Good girl. So sweet when you listen. I'm warning you to play nice with me—" he pauses his ministrations. "I'll make it worth your while. Third time's the charm? I am Julian, and you are—"

"Lupe," I croak, carefully gauging his reaction. He doesn't snicker or laugh. He doesn't raise an eyebrow and mention Diego.

He just nods. "Pleased to meet you. Would you like to form an *alliance* with me, Lupe?"

He makes that word sound so dangerous my entire body quakes.

"I don't know, Jaguar," I mutter, avoiding his latest attempt with the rag. "If it means getting up close and personal again with your friend, Gatita, I think I'll have to pass."

He chuckles and deliberately presses the rag against my temple. "Oh, chica. Being my ally means being under my protection. From Braulio. From anyone who would seek to harm you. Your family would become my family and vice versa."

And Franco would be in his orbit, a tool at his discretion. It's funny how that only sinks in now. And behind it all, Diego will be pulling the strings, of course.

I know better than to refuse him outright. I do what I've excelled at doing—I play along.

"Even my son?"

"Even your son," he echoes, but his voice isn't what I expect. It's not the gallant, suave boast of a savior. It's harsh. The promise of a man who intends to back it up with bloodshed. "But I demand loyalty in return, Tiena. Not the bullshit arrangement you had with Braulio—"

"Braulio didn't deserve my trust. Do you?"

He tilts his head, meeting my stare directly. "I don't think you'd be here if you didn't believe that I do," he replies. "You don't strike me as a fool, *Tiena*. Considering that you attempted to demonstrate so vividly that you aren't afraid of dying to get your way."

Ah, he didn't like that. Not one damn bit. I took his fun away by claiming the spotlight. Unlike Diego, he doesn't seem inclined to punish me for the insolence. On second thought, he's more intrigued than enraged. I've drawn his interest.

"I'm sure you can imagine the benefits of having me on your side. Take those fantasies of yours and times them by two. I can be a very, very good friend to you," he says.

As dazed and exhausted as I am, I still know there's a catch.

"And what do you want?"

"Tell me everything you know about Braulio."

As he himself groused, *again with Braulio.* He has yet to mention Diego's name. Could it be that he truly isn't aware of the specter even his enemy seems to fear?

I take a risk and hope that he isn't.

"No more than you do, I'm sure," I lie. "He must be taking his marching orders from someone big."

"If you don't know anything, Tiena, I have to admit that I don't know why else he'd want to kill you."

He's right. Braulio wouldn't give a damn about one of his girls fucking someone else. He'd just move on. So, I don't draw on him for a frame of reference. Jaguar may know the man peripherally, but a woman involved with a man learns him intimately. Secrets no one else would discern, and to some men, that nearness is lethal. It's poisonous.

"I belong to him. There is no better reason," I say. God, I mean that in the worst possible way. Diego drove that belief into me through years of terror and violence. "How could he let me go to someone else?"

"Well…" Jaguar withdraws his rag, and I note a few smears of scarlet staining the once-white material. "I don't share what's mine, chica. You have nothing to fear from Braulio as long as you're with me."

The promise resonates with the long-suppressed part of me that scoffs in response. He can't own what has already been destroyed and claimed by someone else.

But if it protects Franco in the long run, I can let him believe that.

"I want my son safe. Somewhere far away—"

"I can do better than that, Lupe," Jaguar says, rising to his feet. He extends a hand toward me, and warily I take it. When he tugs me upright, I struggle to regain my balance. In the end, I wind up gripping him too tightly, practically leaning on him for support. I wonder if the shirt I'm wearing is his—it's black, his preferred color.

Without clarifying, he guides me to a window that overlooks the pool, but it's strikingly similar to the one glimpsed from his suite. This room must be beside it.

That suspicion is confirmed when he guides me into the hallway and the familiar suite. I hadn't noticed before, but there are small, personal touches that mark this space as his, one where I suspect few of his posse are allowed inside.

He has me sit on a leather chair beside a desk in an adjoining room. This must be his office.

"We can hammer out the details later," he says, gesturing toward his desk. "There is some work I need to get through first. Can you be a good girl and wait for me?"

My head hurts too badly to argue. As he claims the seat behind his desk, I stand—but I don't go far. I wind up circling around to the window. It's daylight out. I must have been unconscious for hours, but I'm not brave enough to ask exactly how long. This high up, it's even more apparent how reckless and dangerous a stunt jumping was. The scary part?

In my gut, I know that I hadn't been aiming for the pool.

Anger replaces self-pity. After all this time, the mere mention of Diego's name shouldn't have been such a tipping point. He is no longer the center of my universe. Franco is.

"You said you can reunite me with my son," I say softly, shirking Jaguar's request.

He sighs amid the sound of ruffling papers. "Patience, Lupe. Those in my harem like to go play dress-up in the closets. You're free to do so if you can't entertain yourself in my presence."

Ah, a warning. I'm in danger of losing his interest. Which shouldn't matter. A smart woman would probably flounce from his room and find the place furthest away from him. In fact, Pedro would probably vote for that very course of action.

Instead, I pivot on my heel and inspect a nearby row of black shelves sporting various trinkets. There are no books —which I find odd. Not because he's spurned the typical office décor—even Braulio has an entire collection of fake books on display, most doubling as cigar cases—but because I'm sure he has them somewhere. He's hidden them as another way to bolster his mindless brute routine.

"You read," I say, staring at the empty shelves. It isn't a question.

"Do you think I have time while running my empire to thumb through some books, chica?" he counters.

"Oh, I am sure you do," I say, running my fingers along the shelf at eye level. It's pristinely clean, not an ounce of dust. "Will you insult me by lying?"

He laughs. "Men are masters of their own fate, Lupe. What could a book tell me that good old common sense can't?"

It's a harmless enough phrase on its surface, but I feel my eyes widen. When I whirl to face him, he's watching me, an eyebrow cocked in that attentive, cunning way.

"Julius Caesar," I say, naming the source of his clever quote. I read that play twice when I once dreamt of pursuing an education in literature. Diego killed those dreams. "I didn't take you for a Shakespeare man."

His eyebrow jumps a fraction higher. "I think you're mistaken, Lupe."

I'm not. He must be used to coding his words with taunts designed to flaunt his intelligence to those too stupid to recognize it for what it is. A thrill runs down my spine that I can compare only to what I felt with him buried inside me to the hilt. Like I've stumbled upon some elusive, life-changing revelation.

"Do your harem girls fall asleep out of sheer boredom if you talk to them as though they have an ounce of brain left in their skulls? I can assure you that I'm not so shallow."

"I think that after last night you should take very good care of your skull, chica. The doctor says you have a mild concussion," he explains. "Take care with that face, too. I'm sure your past lovers have had to tie you down to keep you from jumping out of windows whenever you don't get your way."

"I always get my way," I lie. It feels better to do so than to admit the obvious. To hide just how vulnerable the falsehood makes me, I turn away from him again, focusing on the wall. Easily overlooked at first glance is what looks like a cabinet built into the gray surface. Perhaps a secret bookshelf? I'm curious enough to approach it and run my finger down the nearly invisible seam.

"Why do you hide your books?" I ask. If he's confident enough to offhandedly quote Shakespeare, I'm sure he's read countless other works. Enough times to remember lines by heart. My personal collection is nowhere near vast, but I still have a few books dog-eared and tattered from how many times I've reread them. If you cherish the written word enough to quote it by heart, you have books. Somewhere.

"What do I need to hide?" Jaguar asks me.

I consider keeping my observations close to the chest—but I suspect he's used to having no one prod at his façade so boldly. After locking me in a cage to be eaten by his pet, I have no scruples about nagging him. Not anymore.

"Your intelligence," I say, hunting for a latch or concealed handle to open the hidden compartment. "I told you before, but I'll say it again. You pretend you're nowhere near as brilliant as you truly are. A dumb man doesn't possess the patience you do."

The cruel, predatory ability to watch and wait. To let people dance for him like puppets because he's *that* convinced he knows exactly how they'll react.

"For example," I press on before he can deny my suspicion outright. "You assumed I'm like the other women you play with. A few pretty dresses and a room filled with makeup would impress me. That my son is merely a footnote on my psyche, and if you promise me the world, I'll simper at your feet while you use me to your own ends. You had no intention of helping me the first time. Will you deny it?"

"And interrupt such a thrilling little monologue?" he rasps. "I think not."

Oh, I've hit him where it counts. Someone smart and well versed in how men like him operate would back down. It seems my head wound has knocked more sense out of me than I thought, because I can't seem to retreat so easily.

"You think hate alone drove me to come to you, but it isn't. If I wanted to destroy Braulio, there are other ways."

Reckless ways, but that doesn't negate their availability.

"I came to you because I don't want revenge. I want protection. Will you believe me now?"

"I don't know what to believe when it comes to you, Tiena. Such a strange, feisty little creature you are."

And that unsettles him. It's yet another glimpse of the real man lurking behind the mask. Even his voice sounds different when he's not putting on the display that is Jaguar. Julian Domingas, I suspect, is someone far more dangerous. He's reasonable, but impressing him takes intellect. Honesty.

So, I switch gears and start speaking to him in Spanish.

"Do you hide your books in the wall?" I ask.

He chuckles more deeply. "I don't feel the need to hide a damn thing." His accent is fluently crisp, his inflection *perfecto*.

Suddenly, the wall parts beneath my fingers—the result of some mechanism he must be able to control from the desk. Via a remote? I start to look over, but what's revealed in the hidden compartment has me too hypnotized to move.

"He's beautiful," I gasp in English.

In lieu of a bookshelf lurks the portrait of a young man, no older than eighteen at the most. His dark brown eyes radiate calm, gentle energy that softens me to him instantly.

"Is he your son?" I don't know how old Jaguar is. His features obscure his age in that he could be anywhere from thirty to fifty.

"He might as well have been," he replies.

I look back to find him sitting forward, his fingers steepled together, his eyes on me instead of the painting. The use of past tense betrays the significance of the portrait. Whoever the boy was, he's now dead.

A silly woman would stumble over herself, rushing to console him. I don't.

"His name?" I ask instead.

He hesitates, though I suspect the dramatic pause isn't for show. He's wondering if I'm worthy of hearing this truth or not. Finally, he murmurs, "Juan."

I look back at the smiling portrait. It's a fitting name, and I wonder about his importance to a man as coldly detached from the world as Jaguar seems. Someone I think even I would find it hard not to like.

"You were close?"

"No," he says, rattling my assumptions. "We were brothers. Family. Few relationships compare to that."

Surprisingly, I recognize a note in his voice that doesn't fit with the harsh persona I've come to know. Pain? It's the same way I speak about Franco, and I know better than to prod for any more details.

To play it safe, I return to the topic of my initial interest. "I'm sure he had a favorite book," I say. "I bet you've kept it."

"Some might find your probing insulting, chica," he scolds. But he isn't angry. Speaking to him on an intellectual level is one of the few times I feel like we're having an actual conversation rather than performing our scripted lines in some grand narco play.

"Give me one of your favorite books to read, and I'll sit here in silence like one of your harem women. I promise." I raise my pinky finger as I turn to face him.

His expression is stone. "Are you calling me a liar, Lupe?"

I choose to remain silent, holding his penetrating stare without flinching. When he reaches for his desk drawer, I'm well aware he could be aiming to grab a gun. What he does wind up tossing onto the desk, however, is a far more dangerous weapon.

It's a tattered, dogeared copy of Macbeth. One so withered with age that I suspect he's reread it more times than he can count. In fact, I have a horrifying sensation that he honored my request to the letter. This book belonged to Juan.

I creep forward and accept it with all the reverence of some holy relic the catholic churches hoard and bring out for special occasions. This is a rare testament to the man behind the mask. I don't think he'll give up another piece of himself without a fight, however.

So, I press this trophy to my chest and eagerly retreat to my vacant chair.

He watches me without a word, his expression stone. Eventually, I sense him return to his documents while I uphold my end of our fragile truce.

I read.

The more I do, the more intrigued I become at the mystery that is this complicated man. He is no mindless brute, and he doesn't read Shakespeare for the supposed culture it endows his image with. The man is all wit and twisted banter, even in the supposed gifts he bestows. I've never met anyone so sadistic who has yet to lay a hand on me himself.

"You're frowning, Lupe," he says once a few hours have passed in silence, as promised. "Is that book not stimulating enough for you?"

"Oh, I find it *very* stimulating," I murmur, looking up. For some reason, I can't stop stroking the edges of the pages. They're worn and ravaged to the point of clinging to the binding by a thread. "You've insulted me so damn cleverly that I don't know how I'll ever return the favor."

"Oh?" His dangerous smirk reappears. "Insulted you? But I've rewarded you, chica. I gave you what you asked for."

"You gave me a warning," I counter, still cradling the worn book in my lap. While I can clearly see the gesture for what it is now, I still can't deny the awe I feel toward this small little paperback. He could have given me a million dollars in cash, and I doubt it would be half as valuable to him. But he isn't all sentimental. He wanted to see if I had the sense to literally read between the lines. "Macbeth," I add. "The tale of a man led astray by the ambition of a dangerous, reckless woman. I'm touched you think so highly of me, Jaguar."

"That's a hell of a way to read into me merely giving you a book, chica," he says with a dismissive laugh. For a second, I almost believe him. He's convincing in his show of arrogance. He must be used to throwing anyone off the scent in this way.

"You don't fool me," I say softly, gently closing the book in my grasp. "I will, however, take your warning with a grain of salt. It's a good thing we aren't married. You would never take my advice, anyway."

"Spicy girl," he says, returning his attention to his documents. "If you've grown bored of needling me, I have six rooms and six closets filled with pretty clothes and expensive makeup. You should go make friends with the others in my harem. It's what you wanted after all, isn't it?"

"I'll tell you what I want. Do this for me, and I'll forgive you for toying with me before."

He chuckles. "Let me guess. A nice pair of shoes? A dress all to yourself? Money? We *share* here, chica. None of my girls have anything here with their name on it."

Because none of them matter to him enough to draw his favor individually.

"Take me to your library," I say. "I know you must have one. Let me spend the day there instead."

"Again, with your foolish assumptions. You're squandering my patience, Lupe. You have such a pretty face to look at, too, but I think I'll have to suffer through my work without your presence. Get out."

I obey without comment, though it pains me to leave his book behind. I wander back into my nearby room and find it empty.

Not even ten minutes later, a shadow darkens the doorway. "Come," Horatio commands, his expression cold.

My heart pangs. Perhaps I went too far. He'll take me to Gatita's cage, I'm sure.

I don't fight, though. I let him lead me downstairs and then to a lower level. Without faltering, I hold my head high and brace myself for the inevitable.

"You are to stay here," Horatio says, opening a large black door.

I steel myself to find Gatita's private room, complete with mauled remains of her owner's enemies. Instead…

My eyes go wide, and I can't silence a gasp of surprise. He has a library, after all. It isn't fancy or a sprawling oasis of literature like one might find in a University. Oh no. This one is entirely his, and I get the sense that no one else comes in here. There's a sacred way he's arranged the various tomes on many shelves. They're packed to bursting with several excess stacks piled on the floor.

There is another desk in here, but it's oddly devoid of anything but a few pens. I recognize the sight. Once upon a time, when I devoted myself to my studies, I kept my desk the same way. So that I could spread out with my books at a moment's notice and dive in.

His mind is a terrifying thing to try and picture. I can visualize him grabbing his latest read and fishing a notebook from his desk. The curiosity is too great, and even while Horatio watches, I cross over to the polished surface and wrench open a drawer.

God, he has good taste in notebooks. They're leather-bound, the kind I would have killed for back in my study days. His pens are of the same quality , and I'm opening the topmost journal before I can stop myself.

Dios mío, his handwriting. It's ruthlessly neat, each word carefully crafted. He didn't take the time to write personal musings or inner thoughts. These are annotations—notes on what he's been reading, with page numbers, dates, and even the time.

"You are to stay here," Horatio repeats, but I barely hear him. I think he even locks me in, but I'm too spellbound to care. I'm a kid in a candy store, intoxicated by the wealth of knowledge of the world and his thought process that he's let me feast upon.

The reality is that Shakespeare makes up a small fraction of Jaguar's literary interests. He has books on everything from weather patterns and geography to classical art. Some I suspect are merely to feed his fleeting curiosities, but a picture of his true passions quickly becomes apparent.

He loves to study people. He has several books on psychology and biology, with both subjects making up the bulk of his annotated notes. He's delved into everything from mental disorders to the various muscles and bones that make up the human body. The next most visited topic? Philosophers. He prefers Aristotle of all people, as well as other influential figures from history.

And I'm impressed. I don't want to be, but sometime during my perusal of the third notebook, my feelings toward him change. The wall of hostility cracks, and for a second, I know I would give anything to watch him sit in this spot and devour his latest read.

As if the desire drew him here, I hear a quiet thud from the doorway. When I look over, he's leaning against the frame, his gaze on me.

"Horatio said you looked upon the shelves like the other women in my harem do the closets. I wanted to see for myself." He doesn't like to divulge that. He is a man who rarely admits his regrets, let alone to another person.

I set my current conquest aside and watch him. Although he holds himself in the same self-assured, arrogant manner I'm used to, there's a slight difference I almost miss. He doesn't take his eyes off me once. He's uneasy letting me into this space.

My awe is unrestrained.

"If you had shown me this the first night, I wouldn't have needed your cock to orgasm," I say, utilizing his naughty language against him. "The shock alone from realizing you have a brain in your skull would have made me come. Talk dirty to me with more of your favorite quotes, and I'll show you a real performance you won't forget."

He laughs, but his eyes narrow in that warning way. He has his guard up, but not entirely.

"How do you know this place is mine and not Horatio's?"

That's easy. I hold up the notebook. "Because you write like you talk. In code. Like you think that revealing the slightest hint of your intellect will draw undo notice. So, you are brief. Succinct. I'd love to hear you explain them to me one day."

He advances and holds out his hand for the notebook, which I relinquish. After scanning the open page, he slams it shut.

"I let you see my books. I never said you could read them or anything else in this room."

I'd shiver at his tone if I didn't see the slight quirk on his upper lip. Sparing verbally with him takes immense skill. After a few sentences, I feel like I've run a marathon, but I can't deny the rush he gives me. It's been so long since I've felt like someone was listening—truly listening—to my every word.

Such attention makes me reckless.

"Let me see more, and I'll make it up to you."

His smirk widens though those eyes never lose their cold hue. "How so?"

"I'll let you in on one of my secrets."

He says nothing, and I'm sure he suspects I'll reveal something about Braulio he can use to his benefit. Maybe if

I knew something of the sort, I'd tell him. Instead, all I have deals with me.

"Fucking you was what made me see it," I blurt, taking a risk by speaking first. "How you hide the real you."

"Oh?" He braces a calloused hand against the desk's surface and leans in. "And how so? Was my magic cock really that good? I'm used to flattery, chica, but damn. You certainly know how to ladle it on."

"And genuine praise makes you uncomfortable. Not because you don't believe you deserve it. You think I'm winding you up."

"And are you?" he asks, flicking his gaze over my exposed front. "Do tell."

"I'm not. But you don't trust me. You think I was faking it the first time, but I wasn't."

And perhaps that's a step too far when it comes to honesty. Being in this room does something to me. It lowers the iron wall I've learned to keep up—and not just when it comes to him. Diego trained me well, and maybe the threat of him unravels my armor now.

"You don't hide yourself when you fuck someone. You're brutal and unrestrained, and you don't give a damn if your partner enjoys it. You let them get a glimpse of the real you, and if they only want pretty clothes and shoes, then it's their price to pay. You don't force them, but you don't work for their approval, either."

Other men are different. They thrive on praise wrung from eager mouths, and they need to feel like a big man. He would have preferred it if I had played the same song and dance with him. Not because it would get him off but because it would minimize me as a threat.

"You don't believe anyone could enjoy the real Julian, but I did. It's why you don't trust me."

His expression doesn't reveal if my hunch is correct or not. "I think I'm beginning to realize that you enjoy reckless, dangerous stunts, chica. But you forget one thing. One aspect of our fucking that I would like clarity on, *sí?*" Without warning, he captures my chin in one hand. "You commanded me. Go slow, remember? Why would a woman who enjoyed my cock so much beg me to take her gently? One might assume I hurt you."

He utters the statement as though it were a trump card. Concrete proof that I was lying. He couldn't be more wrong.

"I wanted to feel you," I confess, my voice huskier than I mean it to be. "And you let me. No one ever has before."

I'm referring to just one man, but he doesn't need to know that. In any case, the point is the same.

"You gave me a taste of control, yet you didn't hold back. You didn't demand I take you as you wanted. You gave me what I asked for, even in that small way, and it…"

Turned me on like nothing else. Even now. I've grown wet just thinking of him, and that terrifies me. Honesty aside, I pray he didn't enjoy my body the same way. Avoiding another tryst with him would be in my best interest.

I can't risk getting attached to him. Or addicted.

"And if I were to fuck you now around your precious books?" Jaguar asks, putting my personal vow in utter peril. "How wet would you be?"

Embarrassingly so. I've never been this aroused. Ever. My body reacts to his presence in ways I can't deny, even though I know I should be alarmed by the intensity of it all. This man will be the death of me.

It's a good thing I'm already legally deceased, then.

I don't know who moves first. I think he flexes his hand to guide me out of my seat, but I'm already standing. He doesn't let me circle the desk, however. He leans over it and hooks his hands beneath my waist, yanking me on top of the wooden surface so I'm resting on my knees. In a graceful display of strength, he extends my legs before me and steps between them.

He moves to free his cock, but I stop him by reaching for his fly first. A thrill shoots down my spine that I can't deny. I feel like a child unwrapping the most coveted present on Christmas morning. The comparisons between him and Diego threaten to overwhelm me, but one sticks out.

I never rushed to undress him first. He would never allow it, and it wasn't long before sex with him became a punishment. A necessary task he had to undertake to cement his hold over me. I never ached for him. I never felt my body practically vibrate for his touch, and I never understood what it meant to be wet. Truly wet.

It's frightening how aroused I feel, and Jaguar hasn't even touched me in the ways that matter. He watches me through heavy-lidded eyes and raises his hands so that I can tackle his fly unassisted. When I get him free, my mouth goes dry.

God, he's beautiful. He's terrifying. His cock is a weapon composed of flesh and straining veins, and rock-hard muscle. He seems to be feeling the equivalent of what I am, swollen to a painful degree. An unexpected impulse rises within me—I want to taste him. Badly. I want to feel what it's like to have him unleash that power in my mouth.

But not tonight. He winds his fingers through my hair instead, wrenching me toward him. Our lips meet, and in the back of my mind, I realize it's for the first time. We haven't kissed before, but tasting him…

It's an entirely different sensation from riding his cock. His lips are surprisingly soft, navigating mine with a gentleness that catches me off guard. I let him in deeper than I mean to, tilting my head to chase his unique flavor.

A deep sound rumbles in his throat. A warning? His eyes flash with a manic gleam when he withdraws from the kiss.

"I knew you were a woman who liked to kiss," he tells me, but his tone reveals he doesn't intend that as a compliment. "All the better for you to hook your claws into a man, eh, Lupe?"

"Men like you love kissing because it gives you power," I breathlessly counter. "You relish being unattached and unclaimed. You're merely going through the motions."

I lean in, feeling bold enough to tease him further.

"Because if you kissed the way you fuck, you probably would have bitten me."

His eyes narrow at the suggestion, and I get the sense that he agrees. His hand palms my thigh, easing them further apart.

"I'm not into foreplay," he grates, and I take my cue, guiding him into my hand.

He lets me pretend I'm in control right up until the moment I steer him toward my entrance. The second he feels me against his tip, he bucks, and he's so deep my head rears back at the sensation.

"Neither am I," I manage to choke out. With him, fondling isn't necessary. I'm already ready, and I doubt any foreplay could make him feel better than he already does. I think the fact that he's dropped part of his charade makes every inch of him all the sweeter. There is no need for pretense between us.

No more lies.

But the one thought that makes me already near orgasm before he even starts to move? This will be the last time. I'll leave after this. Julian Domingas will become a blur on the periphery of my twisted life and join the number of fucked-up men I've tangled with.

It doesn't matter that I ride him with abandon like a woman possessed.

It doesn't matter that his groans ignite that deep-seated, hidden place within me that only he has ever touched.

It doesn't matter that the pleasure that rams into me is one-hundred percent real, and my moans aren't faked as I writhe against the desk.

All that matters is that I'm in control of my own fate once again.

What a damn good feeling that is.

CHAPTER THIRTEEN

Jaguar hisses as he pulls out of me, his eyes on the mess glistening on the desk's surface beneath us.

"I never fuck in here," he says, but his tone is low with genuine irritation. That confession alone reveals so much about him—he keeps his sexual partners in pre-approved areas of the house, leaving other spaces off-limits. I'm intrigued.

Enough that I don't immediately make an excuse to escape, as I should.

"Don't tell me I made you act impulsively," I quip, drawing my knees together.

His eyes cut to mine, devoid of any humor. "Ah, not in the slightest, chica. You merely gave me my prize before I even saw fit to give you your present. Here."

He withdraws a cell phone from his pocket and angles the screen toward me.

One glance at the headline displayed on it, and my blood goes cold.

"It seems there was a bit of a mess at Braulio's California mansion earlier tonight," Jaguar narrates. "The house was set on fire. Three dead—but, suspiciously, not by smoke inhalation. They were executed, one shot to the skull at point-blank range. The police are keeping that part out of the press for now."

I barely hear him. No… God, no. I just see poor Franco burned and gone because of me. It's like the world has been swept from beneath my feet. I sink to my knees, weightless.

"You seem disappointed," Jaguar scolds with a knowing laugh.

All I can do is gape up at him. Then I muster what little strength I have left, and I lunge. "You son of a bitch."

This was the real source behind his amusement when he found me here earlier. Not because I was in his precious inner sanctum, but because I had been stupid enough to trust him as he ripped my life apart.

"I could kill you—"

"Easy," Jaguar warns, his tone a fraction sharper. He grips my wrist and wrestles me to a stop, but he doesn't go further than that. "No need for threats. I still haven't given you your surprise. Here." He adjusts his phone again, but this time when he holds it out to me, it's in the process of video calling someone who has yet to pick up.

Diego?

I stiffen as a face comes into view, but…

"Francisco!" I grab the phone , and Jaguar relinquishes it, letting me retreat to the furthest corner away from him. "Baby, are you okay?"

"Mama?" He sounds confused, but I nod and plead with my eyes for him to play along.

"I've missed you so much. Are you okay? Where are you?"

He looks to his left.

"Somewhere safe," Jaguar says from behind me. "No need to worry about the details just yet. I've arranged for him to be taken someplace far from any chaos. Say goodbye for now. You will speak again when he's at his destination."

"I love you," I tell him. "Don't be afraid. Trust me. I will never let anything happen to you, I promise."

He nods, and far too soon, the call ends.

Eyes blazing, I whirl on Jaguar. "Is this all a game to you? Traumatize a child to prove a point?"

"I'm not above it," he admits, taking the phone from me. "But in this instance, Tiena, I wasn't the one who launched the attack. Which brings me to a very good question. Who did and why? You seem to have plenty of enemies, chica. Braulio cares for the boy, but if anyone wanted leverage against the bastard, they would kidnap him. Not kill."

But I know someone who wouldn't give a damn either way.

"You've gotten my attention," Jaguar says. "Let's hope neither one of us regrets it."

"What does that mean?" I demand. "You continue to yank me around, demanding answers?"

"No." Gone is any playfulness in his expression. He's the cold, calculating figure lurking behind the sadistic narco mask. "It means it's time for you to get Braulio out of your head, *Tiena*. I'm taking you up on your initial offer—so you better make plenty of room in that skull for *me*." He slips his forefinger into his mouth, and I belatedly realize it's the same one he touched me intimately with just minutes prior. As my cheeks flame, I tell myself that disgust is the cause. "I've decided you might be a worthwhile toy to play with after all."

I flinch. Any other time I would interpret those words the way I should—as a dangerous, blaring warning sign. The last thing on earth that I need is another Diego...

"You don't look pleased," Jaguar scolds. "I thought this was what you wanted, Tiena? Me, the man you so eagerly pledged your pussy to."

"I pledged it to the man I *thought* Jaguar was," I blurt out. His eyes flash in that unsettling way, but it's too late. I can't play the game anymore. Not with very real consequences on the line. Having him toy with me is one thing. But he doesn't seem to be joking now. I need to know what's truly at stake. "I don't know the first damn thing about Julian Domingas."

He cocks his head. "Don't you?" As he advances, a barrage of guttural laughter rumbles from his chest, easily cornering me against the nearest bookshelf. He reaches out, palming my cheek with one hand. "You were smart enough to see through my bullshit act. To notice my 'intelligence,' as you call it. To expose me to my fucking face. No one ever has, little Lupe. You can take pride in that."

Admiration isn't what I find in his gaze. Anger is. For the first time, he lets me see how irritated he is by my constant needling. I've seen through his façade, but not because he allowed me to.

"You think that makes you smart. Sexy." He strokes along my jawline until he can seize a fistful of my hair—hard. He tugs on the mass, bringing my face inches from his. "It doesn't. It makes you a liability. A threat. You claim to see through me so easily, but I can see through you. A woman living under an assumed name who is nothing like what she should be. I don't mean that as a compliment either—" He wrenches me closer, his teeth bared, breath hot on my throat. "The supposed whore who feels like a fucking virgin. The supposed calculator who can't decipher the most basic fucking numbers presented before her. A stone-cold man-eater who betrays a bastard she is still in love with." His nostrils flare excitedly as I feel all the color drain from my face.

"Oh yes, Tiena," he breathes. "You thought I couldn't see it? You put on a good act, but it's written all over you for those who know what to look for. The way you flinch at my touch. The faraway look in your eyes. The way you jump at the mere mention of him…"

I hold my breath, prepared for the inevitable. He lied to me—he's been working with him all along. *Diego.*

"Braulio," Jaguar says. I blink, confused. Another mind game? No. His expression is far too serious. "He has your soul on a leash, chica. You flaunt yourself like you can be won, but you've already been bought and sold. You have no interest in anyone else. Do you want to know what gave you away?"

He presses into me, heedless of my back. With my resolve already rattled, I can't silence a whine. Fear ratches up, constricting the air in my lungs. Will he hurt me?

He raises his hand, and I recoil against the hard spines of the books, bracing for impact. My face isn't where his fingers finally land, however.

He grips my inner thigh instead, aiming for the flesh still slick with his seed.

"*I don't do foreplay.* You were so relieved when I said that." He chuckles, his eyes gleaming. "*Too* relieved. No woman in the world enjoys sex without getting her fair share, and if there is one thing I am not, it's selfish."

He gives to me now, working a finger inside me. My head rears back. I'm still sore from the last time, overly tender. If he was too rough, it would hurt—knowing that puts his actual gentleness into stark relief. He eases inside of me, letting my body do the real work to coax him deeper.

Everything I thought I knew about Julian Domingas is undermined by this earth-shattering experience. No one has touched me so tenderly. No one.

"I always repay my debts, Lupe. I told you that once." He releases my hair but brings his face in closer, brushing his lips against my ear. "And I am no fool. Sex is a chore for you, isn't it? Your heart isn't in it. You can make yourself orgasm, but it's greedy. Reckless. Stingy. You can separate yourself from me. There is one problem, though, Lupe. I don't want a *piece* of you—"

Another finger enters me alongside the first. Another. In unison, he guides them in and out of me. Then he crooks one, and I cry out. The pleasure hits me hard, too harsh—an overdose of ecstasy, but only a mere taste of what I know him to be capable of.

"I will have *all* of you. Tell me now if that isn't on the table."

It isn't. It shouldn't be. I sold my soul to someone once and swore never to do so again.

"No," I start to say, but somewhere in the process of forcing the answer from my throat, he moves those fingers again. They spread apart. Curl together. Press against my inner walls and strain the muscles eager to clamp down over them.

Dios mío. I gasp for air, gaping up at the ceiling. He thinks love for Braulio is the reason why I claimed to be disinterested in foreplay, but the truth is...

I've never experienced it. Diego never touched me like this. He never felt me drip around his fingers. He never wanted me willing.

And he never took my natural responses as a challenge.

"Look at me... Look." Jaguar wraps his hand around my neck slowly, letting me adjust to the weight of every last finger. If he squeezed until my eyes bulged, I could interpret the gesture for what it must be—a threat. Instead, he cradles my throat like a living, breathing, necklace. Or a collar.

"Braulio fucked you senseless, but I want more than your pretty moans and gushing orgasms." He takes me with him as he walks backward, steering me toward the desk. Then he shoves me onto it face down.

I wince as pain rips through my back, but it's dull in comparison to what it could be—and even as I tense, his hand lands on my ass, rubbing at the flesh to soothe the sting.

"You thought you weaseled a secret out of me with the books, but you didn't." His hand withdraws, and heavy footsteps echo as he retreats from me. I scramble to turn, tracking his movement across the room to one of the bookshelves. He runs his finger along the spine of a leather volume and removes the book entirely, flipping it open to some random page. With his eyes on the text, he returns to me, his pace slow and deliberate. "I found you worthy of knowing that little tidbit of information, so I shared it willingly. You had the balls to call it as you saw it. I can respect that. Count yourself lucky. Few can say the same. *That* is the kind of man Julian Domingas is—" His gaze bores into me, slicing through flesh and bone. "He rewards those who refuse to lie down and die. You aren't the little doe-eyed fool you pretend to be. No, you are every bit as fierce as my Gatita. Aren't you?"

The desk vibrates as he tosses his book onto it, placing it within my reach.

"Now I want you to read again for me. Nice and loud." He's gone again before I can process the command—but he doesn't go far. My legs are nudged apart to make way for a firm mass to step between them.

"Open it," Jaguar commands in a tone like iron. His hands rake down my hips and cup my ass before heading lower. "I earmarked the page for you. Now, Tiena."

Still in his grasp, I scramble for the book, too dazed to argue. He earmarked the page alright, but I realize this is no ordinary book. It's a Bible.

"The highlighted section, read it for me," Jaguar says—only I feel his breath on parts of me I shouldn't. My core is on fire, the flesh raw and aching. Every word he speaks feels like fire from a blowtorch.

I writhe, straining the pages in my grasp.

"I won't commence with our lesson until you read," Jaguar snaps. "You should be eager to. It's my vow to you. From this moment on, you remember every fucking word of it."

Of what? My eyes threaten to roll at another dangerous taste of his heat—and he hasn't even touched me. It isn't until I finally read that I feel his fingers inching along my inner folds.

Somehow, I force out the words. With every one, I gain a disturbing understanding of what he meant. "Ask, and it will be g-given—"

"*Sí.*"

A moan rips out of me as delicious wet warmth engulfs me in one go. My brain can't even process the act for what it *must* be. Only a few things in the world have those devious qualities. His tongue. His mouth. His raking, nipping teeth.

All at once, the sensation withdraws. "I told you to read," comes a grated command.

To comply, I fight to suck in air. "Given to you... *Dios mío.*"

"Ask, and it shall be given to you," he says. The next second, a stiff ridge of flesh worms its way inside me, and I lose focus of everything but screaming nerves and vicious friction. He doesn't work me like he did with his fingers.

He devours me, inside and out, like he's a predator and my only purpose is to be his prey.

Desperate, I paw at the surface beneath me and wind up batting the book away. When he retreats, the disappointment I feel is harrowing. My lips part. "Don't—"

"Seek, and you will find," he recites. Then more pressure. More tasting. More him. "Knock—"

It shouldn't be possible so soon, but I'm orgasming again, caught beneath a tidal wave of sensation. I can't breathe. Can't think. Somehow though, I can still hear him, relentless in his narration.

"Knock, and the door will be opened to you," he says into me. "Remember that. I am a man of my word, Tiena."

Tiena. Her name rings in my brain like a warning bell toll, outlasting even the ravages of ecstasy. I tense, and damn near instantly, he pulls away, rising to his feet.

For a second, he paces, raking his hands through his short hair while I watch, too breathless to move.

"I could fuck you now," he finally tells me, his voice grated and thick. "Taste you again. Bend you over the table and show you what you've been missing. What that bastard has denied you. But I don't waste my gifts on the unwilling, Tiena. You want to be mine? Prove it to me." He returns to the desk and shoves my legs together, so suddenly I gasp at the shocking emptiness left behind. Then he stands back, tugging at the collar of his shirt. "I'll give you a day," he snaps, storming for the door. "Go. Horatio will take you home. Get out."

He's gone before I have the presence of mind to regain control of my breathing. When I do, a watchful figure stands in the doorway.

"I take you home now, Miss," Horatio says sternly.

My clothing, or lack thereof, doesn't seem to matter to him. He ushers me unceremoniously through the house and into a spacious garage containing over a dozen luxury cars. His choice is a plain, black sedan, and moments later, I'm before Pedro's apartment—only Horatio doesn't seem content to let me enter the building alone.

He parks in an underground garage and follows me up a service elevator and straight into my apartment. Only at the door does he seem content to let me out of his sight.

"A day," he says, parroting Jaguar's deadline. "You contact him when ready."

He retreats, and when I finally wrestle the door closed, I lock it. Then I brace my weight against it and sink to the floor, too stunned to move. Whatever drug his doctor supplied me with is wearing off. I feel every ache and pain. My back hurts worst of all. The skin feels itchy and inflamed. Infected?

The potential health complications are the least of my worries, however.

When I finally have the sense to scan the rest of the apartment's interior, I note that something feels...off. The furniture is as I left it, the curtains drawn shut over the windows—but there is a smell in the air I don't recall noticing before.

It's sharp, like vinegar, and yet sweet like cologne. A unique smell that itches at my brain as though I should recognize it. I know this smell. But how?

Confused, I stand and find myself blindly following its invisible trail, through the kitchenette and down the hall, into the bedroom.

This space is not as I left it. The bed has been neatly made and adorned with what I assume are giant, misshapen sequins at first. Hundreds of them are coating the beige comforter and dotting the floor.

One step closer brings what they are into clearer focus, however.

Not sequins—butterflies. Real ones, all of them dead.

All of them grim reminders of a past I thought I'd left behind.

God, I can even hear his voice, cruel and smug. *I'm back, my little butterfly. Did you miss me?*

Diego.

Diego.

Diego.

And all I can do is scream.

CHAPTER FOURTEEN

A lot can change in a blink of an eye. The people you once trusted can become enemies, and your enemy...

He might be your only comfort once the tables turn. The sad part is that I never intentionally seek out Julian Domingas.

He comes running to me. Much like a predator sensing bleeding, dying prey. He's ravenous, and I make for an easy meal.

"Horatio." His voice proceeds him into my borrowed apartment, sharp with alarm. As he storms in through the front door, he cuts a striking figure against the beige interior. Only God knows how he got here so fast. Did he follow after I left with Horatio? From his expression alone, I can't tell. "Status?" he calls out.

"Yes, Sir." Horatio approaches him, inclining his head with a wary glance toward me. The relative emptiness of this room allows their words to echo, and I catch bits of their conversation, though they speak in low voices.

"No sign of forced entry," Horatio says. "No witnesses. They did leave this…"

Both men retreat down the hall while I remain on the couch, locked inside my own mind. It's funny how I can see a grown man torn apart by an exotic animal and maintain my composure. I didn't break then.

But the sight of a few dead insects shatters me. I can't escape what they symbolize—who they symbolize—a broken shell of a woman I thought I'd left behind.

"*Ay, Dios mío.* It seems Braulio isn't happy with you, Tiena," Jaguar says, his voice rasping with amusement and irritation. He must enjoy seeing me like this, and yet… His frustration comes from the fact that another man can easily accomplish what he failed to do.

I can't even hide my genuine fear. My eyes are burning, my face damp with tears that won't stop falling no matter how hard I try to suppress them.

"He'll never let me go," I hear myself say in a voice so broken it's barely coherent. The statement isn't for dramatic effect. It's simply a reminder of what I've spent the past decade trying to ignore.

Braulio isn't the man with his hooks into me—Diego Mendez is.

And he will never let me go.

"We'll see about that," Jaguar says. His tone yanks me from the depths of fear long enough that I can observe his face for the first time. His smirk is in place, his face half-shrouded in shadow. "For now, I think you might be safer staying someplace else."

"I'll find one," I say, preempting any suggestion on his part that I stay in his mansion among his harem. I'll find a way to reach Pedro and see if he can help me find somewhere else to stay. Poor Pedro. I'll have to tell him about Diego.

"I am sure your skills for finding real estate rival your skills of seduction, Lupe," Jaguar says. "But I'll have to respectfully disagree. Don't forget the bargain you made, chica. You pledged yourself to me, and I intend to fully protect my investment."

I cringe at that. "By keeping me among the rest of your pretty dolls?" I ask.

He laughs, but cocks a dark eyebrow in surprise. "You don't sound very eager, Lupe. One might think that you aren't worried about Braulio getting his hands on you, after all."

I shake my head, compelled to explain. "Hiding won't matter."

Even Jaguar can't keep me safe. He'll tire of me eventually, and the specter of Diego will be waiting. I've grown bored of playing the role of a trapped animal. I'd rather get my torment over with.

"Have some faith," Jaguar scolds in a tone that makes me shiver. "After all, I wouldn't want to think this was all a ploy to garner my sympathy..."

I interpret the statement for what it is—a warning. Any other time, I think I'd react to it and rush to placate him. *Yes,* I need him as an ally. *Yes,* I need him to secure my nephew—who he thinks is my son. Mere hours ago, those concerns were at the forefront of my mind.

But fear is an old friend, one I find hard to shake.

Did you miss me, butterfly? Diego's voice echoes in my skull, rasping and gleeful. *I've missed you...*

In retrospect, it's hard to remember what I saw in him. Our first meeting wasn't particularly remarkable. My twin sister was too busy chasing narcos to pay her way, and I had no choice but to take whatever odd jobs I could. One of them was selling keychains to tourists for a grumpy old man who ran his operation out of a gas station.

One of those men seemed like an American at first, with haunting green eyes and golden hair. Diego, he said his name was. He spoke in beautiful Spanish and told me I had a sexy little smile.

Like a young, dumb fool, I let him talk me into meeting him after my shift.

And my world was forever changed. For the next year, Diego Mendez became my entire universe, and I nearly died trying to escape him.

"Are you listening to me, Lupe?" Jaguar demands. He cups my cheek, stroking away an errant tear. "If you don't want to be tucked amongst my other dolls, I will humor you. But you will come with me. Horatio will secure your things." He heads for the door, expecting me to follow.

I can't move.

Is he watching me now, Diego? Was he really here, or was this display merely a trick played on me by the few people in my life who know the truth? I can't even decide which outcome would be harder to face.

"Lupe." Jaguar's voice ripples with authority, but I note that it's marginally softer. He isn't angry anymore. He's curious. "Come."

I attempt to stand and feel my knees buckle as the abuse done to my body chooses now to assault me at full force. My head hurts so bad, my back on fire, my hip bruised and sore. I trip and grabble for the arm of the couch for stability.

It isn't necessary. A gentle force captures my waist and tethers me to a body that feels chiseled from stone.

"Easy," Jaguar murmurs near my ear. "Braulio won't like it if there is nothing left of you to come after, will he?"

His laughter echoes mockingly, but even I don't miss the subtle possession laced within that tone. Julian Domingas has made up his mind about what he wants from me, it seems. Even his touch feels different. He tugs me into him and then lifts me into his arms when my knees fail to hold me upright.

He'll take whatever bit of my soul is left, and he doesn't intend to share it.

I don't feel comforted in the least. I regret chasing after him at all. Diego had no choice but to let me go when I fought back.

But Jaguar? I think he'd gladly take up the challenge of haunting me.

CHAPTER FIFTEEN

He has a strange sense of humor, Jaguar. As predicted, he brings me back to his mansion, but when he instructs Horatio to show me where I'll be staying, I'm not brought to one of the gaudy rooms his harem cohabitate.

Instead, I'm brought to a room on the basement level that resembles a makeshift library. It's changed some since the last time I was in here—only last night, in fact. The books themselves have been rearranged into slightly neater stacks, and a new bookshelf has sprung from nowhere to contain the volumes that used to be piled on the floor. All to make room for a small cot in the far corner, made up for one person.

The man can be petty when he wants to be, but I don't complain. For the time being, I can't even bring myself to ask about Franco, or if Braulio has been spotted after he attacked me.

I am still stuck in the web that Diego Mendez once wrapped around my entire mind. There is always the possibility that Jaguar is working with him. That they are conspiring together, all to entrap me. I wouldn't put it past them both.

But I am no one's willing pawn. Whether Jaguar wants to play his cards or not, there is one way to get the truth out of him.

"He wants you to stay here," Horatio warns as I turn on my heels at the threshold of the study and head blindly down the hall.

After these past few days, I've become familiar with the house enough to find Jaguar's main haunt—his pool in the heart of the U-shaped villa.

There, his concubines and entourage gather now, lounging throughout the courtyard while their master holds court from the terrace. Pressed to his ear is a cell phone he speaks into while navigating a computer tablet balanced on his lap.

For a second, I forget my intentions for seeking him out and just stare. He is a singular creature whenever he drops the charade of carefree, boisterous narco he hides behind. It's like he transforms into a different person. A hard frown replaces the smirk, and his eyes take on a thoughtful, calculating gleam.

What I wouldn't give to get inside his head. In the small chance that he isn't working for Diego, he might be the only man in the world capable of outsmarting him.

God, the thought terrifies me. No man should be so cunning. Displaying such intelligence now, he flicks those watchful eyes in my direction. Suddenly, I'm aware of how tired I am. How broken. I'm still wearing only the black button-down he sent me home in last night and nothing else.

I haven't even had time to wash him off me.

I reek of Julian Domingas.

With a tilt of his chin, he beckons me closer, robbing me of the chance to approach him uninvited and make a scene. Even if I wanted to, I lack the strength to do so. My legs shake. I can barely walk in a straight line, and I sense Horatio hot on my heels. To show his displeasure at my disobedience of his request, but also to prevent me from falling into the pool.

"I take it that you aren't pleased with your accommodations," Jaguar says to me, his eyes gleaming— but I only have a fraction of his attention. His brows furrow, presumably due to whatever he hears on the other end of the cell phone.

"*Sí*," he snaps. "Call me when you learn more." He hangs up and tucks the device into his pocket. Lips quirked in a grin, he inclines his head toward me.

"I suggest you get settled in, Lupe. You could be here a while."

I don't let myself take the statement as a threat or a warning. I just approach him, half-naked and exhausted, with my eyes bloodshot from tears.

Chuckling, he steadies my waist enough to help me mount his lap, knocking the tablet aside. I glance at the screen for a second—it looks like a real estate website page displaying a modern mansion.

"This is a surprise," Jaguar murmurs, drawing my attention back to him. "You were so distraught earlier I was afraid we might have to sedate you."

And I will forever hate myself for displaying that weakness. The odd part is that if Diego were watching me... That display alone should have been enough to draw him out. No worries. I know what definitely will.

Without an ounce of restraint, I capture Jaguar's face in both hands and press my mouth to his. My heart skips a beat, betraying the true motive behind such a reckless act. Fear.

Jaguar taunted me that I liked to kiss the last time we had sex—but he didn't know the full truth, and I cringe to admit it inside my own head. Diego was my only sexual partner, but fucking wasn't what he primarily utilized to assert control over me.

Kissing was.

He would do so brutally, biting me hard enough to draw blood. *I'm the only man who can taste you like this,* he'd say.

Even if he were working with Jaguar, he could never stomach such a direct insult. Never. He would storm out of hiding and do more than leave dead butterflies for me to find. He would punish me.

And I doubt Jaguar would do so in full view of witnesses if he knew the man. Rather than pull away, he invites me in, matching the slow, sensual movements of my mouth in his own twisted rhythm.

I stiffen. *This isn't right.*

The second I do, he draws back first and runs his lips from my jaw to my ear. "Ah… You think I don't see what you're doing?" he asks me, his voice a grated rasp. "Oh, Lupe, you yourself claimed that I am smarter than I let on. If a woman who shies at the idea of fucking a man in front of his boys kisses him so openly, affection isn't what she's after. She wants to prove a point. I'll let it slide this one time, but if you suspect me of something, you ask me outright. *Claro?*" he adds, before I can turn away. "If you truly want to continue this conversation, go wait for me in my suite like a good girl. Run along. I will join you shortly."

My face heats at his dismissive tone, but there's another facet to his request that I don't miss. A carefully concealed promise for answers. He saw this ruse for what it was. Perhaps he knows Diego after all, and is unwilling to provoke him outright? Will he tell me if I ask?

Or…

Perhaps in his suite, Diego himself will be waiting for me.

I tell myself that hope isn't what makes me climb off Jaguar and stagger toward the house. Relief is. Finally, we can end this chase here, and I will know for sure whether or not the monster from my nightmares has returned.

If he has, I can face him. I'm ready.

Or not. My steps falter as I mount the stairs inside the air-conditioned villa and near the entrance to Jaguar's private suite. My knees buckle, my breaths shallow. I can't even reach for the doorknob, and I sense—as quiet as ever—Horatio is lurking down the hallway, watching me.

Even if it makes me a coward to hesitate, I don't care. If Diego is here... What will I even say to him after all this time? Will I even get the chance to?

After all, he'll be after only one thing—revenge.

When it comes down to it, I don't have a choice. As advancing footsteps come from the direction of the staircase, I open the door myself. If this is a trap, I won't be blindsided by both men at once. I'll face Diego alone. Only he is entitled to view my initial shock, after all.

As I enter the large lounge area that serves as the first part of Jaguar's interconnected rooms, I find no one waiting for me. Neither is he in the bedroom or the office. A spacious bathroom serves as his lone potential hiding place, but when I tip-toe inside it on trembling legs, I find nothing but polished gray marble and a massive walk-in shower.

Despite the opulence he has on display for his cohorts, Jaguar prefers simplicity, it seems. Harsh colors and sleek modernity. Cold, crisp surroundings.

"I like how you think, Lupe," the man himself remarks in a low rasp as he comes up behind me. "I, too, could use a nice shower."

What feels like his hand nudges my hip, inching me inside so he can close the door behind us. Then he grabs my shoulders and steers me into the shower stall. There, he surprises me by finding the buttons of my borrowed shirt and undoing them one by one.

"I think you're entitled to some pampering after what you've been through," he tells me, his voice unnervingly soft. At the same time, I feel what must be his lips graze my throat in a terrifying caress. "Normally, I would have one of my harem women attend to you, but I don't think you'd like that very much, would you? It seems you think they're beneath you, Lupe."

"I don't," I admit, staring straight ahead at the blank wall before me. "I know better than anyone what it means to be a kept woman. To both preen for and fear the man holding your leash." Real bitterness leeches into my voice. I can't help it.

"Ah, but Braulio kept you well compensated, chica. I've heard the rumors. The houses. The pretty dresses. The cars. You didn't seem too fearful, locked inside your gilded cage."

And maybe Tiena wasn't all that fearful. My captivity, on the other hand, was not so comfortable. Diego didn't supply me with pretty things and endless luxury when he had me. We lived in a tiny one-bedroom apartment in the middle of nowhere, and I would be lucky if he gave me enough money to buy the odd pair of earrings or a book now and again. The truth is, I don't relate to Jaguar's women, and I certainly don't see myself as better than them.

In a way, I think I envy them. Interacting with such a man willingly must employ a skill of endurance that I simply don't have. The fact that Jaguar mentioned them at all brings up an avenue of genuine curiosity I have yet to venture down.

"You're upset with what I did," I say, reading the barely concealed tension in his fingers. "You kiss them in the open, I'm sure. Why not me?"

To be fair, I haven't seen him be affectionate with them. I'm assuming.

"You mean besides the fact that you're barely capable of standing upright?" He laughs as he tosses the shirt outside the shower's glass barrier. Then he begins to strip his own clothing.

I blame delirium for avidly watching him. His body is a thing of perfection.

"Oh no, Tiena, you aren't as slick as you think. That wasn't a kiss—that was provocation. You think Braulio is watching you always. You wanted merely to prove a point to him alone. I was your gun in that instance, to fire the warning shot."

"Because you are working for him." I eye him carefully, awaiting his reaction.

He doesn't even blink. "Now, why the hell would I do a thing like that?" he wonders, letting his pants fall. He steps out of them next and kicks them from the stall. Then he turns to a metal panel built into the wall.

Seconds later, a gentle mist erupts from unseen showerheads.

"To trap me," I tell his back. "To trick me. To give me to him on a silver platter in exchange for more power."

He doesn't rile in anger at having his supposed evil scheme exposed. He chuckles and eyes me with a skeptically raised eyebrow.

"You do have such an elevated sense of importance," he says, returning to me. "Don't think me sexist for saying so, but you aren't the center of the universe, chica. I doubt Braulio would risk going toe to toe with me for *you*."

If only he were right. I'd take comfort in his strange, brutal sense of protection.

But I don't.

I've tried to deny it, but what I saw in the apartment cements my deepest fear. Diego is out there, waiting—and patience was never his strong suit.

"Look up," Jaguar commands, tilting my chin against his palm. As a result, water runs down my forehead, tinged with red.

He got a wash rag from somewhere and lathers it with sweet-smelling soap before washing me in earnest. My mind reels as he drops to his knees and sets about what he must deem as the filthiest place on me—between my legs.

I should feel violated. Instead, my eyelids feel heavy, and my thoughts dissipate. He's unnervingly gentle again. My brain can't process it in this heightened state. Diego is banished for an instant, and it's such a strange feeling.

Because Jaguar infects me in return.

I'm vulnerable to him in a way I rarely am. His voice resonates within me to the core. "I want to know something..."

Ruthless, he chases me into this dreamlike mind state, itching at the fragile peace.

"What?" I ask when he falls silent.

His hand creeps along my thigh in a featherlight caress. Then he strokes me with the rag. Caresses. Strokes.

"Why the butterflies?"

My heart stutters. "Because... Because it's what he called me," I confess, my voice hoarse. His silly, pretty, fragile little butterfly Lupita.

"Oh." Jaguar laughs, but about fractures my distrust of him. He didn't know. Diego surely would have let that detail slip? "That wouldn't be my choice when it comes to you," he adds, furthering that suspicion. "You do seem to think you can fly—" A pointed reminder of when I jumped from a second-floor balcony into his pool the other night. "But you aren't some delicate fluttering creature. No, chica. You have *claws*."

His own nails graze me as I sense him rise to his feet. He moves his rag over my breasts next. Then my throat.

"Either that, or you'd be a slithering little snake. A sexy viper."

I open my eyes and find that his smile has vanished. Those eyes are entirely serious now, and he steps into me, making my pulse surge.

"I'll warn you this once, to show how nice of a man I can be..." He presses his forehead to mine, seeming to nuzzle my cheek. "You forget him. From here on out, I am the only man you concern yourself with. I will accept your bargain, Lupe. You. In return, you belong only to me."

I can't resist needling him just a little. It's the only way I can stay sane. "The piece of you not claimed by those in your harem, you mean."

He doesn't laugh. His hand comes from nowhere, fisting through my hair to hold me captive. His lips slam against mine, but with punishing force. Hungry intensity. Possessive need.

I struggle to keep up, but there is no use. My lip stings, caught between his teeth as he easily wins this round, beating my mouth into submission. Mercilessly, he advances, surging our combined bodies against the wall.

I rip my mouth from his and cry out. My back is in agony —but the pain is nothing compared to the chaos wreaking havoc inside my brain.

"Ah…" Jaguar steps back, but presses his thumb against my lower lip in a quiet warning. "Whether I own one woman or a hundred, you are now one of them. Smile, Lupe. After all, this is what you wanted."

I don't smile as I hold his probing stare and try to find his real motive lurking within it.

"Isn't it, Tiena?"

"No. I don't want your possession," I admit, hating how my voice openly breaks. "I want your protection. Can you promise me that?"

One is fleeting, based on his current whim—but the other? It conveys far more than parading me around as part of his harem. It means in case he isn't working with Diego, he will defend me from him.

No matter the cost.

"I won't promise you a damn thing," he says, his grin unfolding in full. "I'll keep you guessing. No one yanks my chain around here, sweetheart. *You* are the only one on a leash."

And maybe he has a point, but he isn't the one holding the other end of my strings.

Seemingly done washing me, Jaguar shuts off the water and exits the stall, returning seconds later with a towel slung over his waist and another that he tosses to me.

Still dripping wet, I follow him inside his main bedroom and gape as he towels himself off and strolls naked into a massive walk-in closet.

His bimbos must not stay in here. The clothing on the hangers is all masculine, primarily in his chosen shade of black. He dresses in jeans and a leather jacket before tossing an oversized T-shirt to me.

I don't move to put it on. Being here increasingly feels more surreal than my tired brain knows what to do with, but there isn't time to rest. I should call Pedro. I need to get in contact with Franco. I need to know what Braulio meant about Tiena selling him out. I need…

"I want that magic tongue well rested," Jaguar says, intruding upon my thoughts. "You'll need it for what I have in mind. Just this once, I will make another exception for you. You can rest here rather than in one of the other rooms."

He snatches the shirt from me and pulls it over my head himself. Then he takes my hand and leads me to the bed.

"Be a good girl," he warns before I can open my mouth to protest. Displaying that disarming strength again, he makes me lie down and drapes the blankets over me. It's a cruel, demented comparison to a child being tucked in by a doting caretaker. He even settles me on my stomach so I don't aggravate my back.

Then he kisses my cheek.

"Sleep tight, little Lupe," he says before retreating for the door. "Don't let the monsters bite. I am the only one allowed to dwell inside that head of yours. Remember that."

CHAPTER SIXTEEN

It should be impossible for me to find comfort in the bed of a twisted psychopath like Julian Domingas. If anything, I should spend the next few hours tossing and turning, unable to find more than a few snatches of sleep at a time.

The truth is, when I finally peel my eyes open again, the room is dark, and I know in my gut that I slept for hours. Blissful, dreamless, much-needed hours.

Perhaps because my tormentor isn't anywhere to be found? Even in the darkness, I can tell the room is empty apart from me. A gentle orange light emanates from the center courtyard, and I can make out low voices and playful music.

Is he out there, perhaps, lording over those under his purview?

I try not to care. Sleep has cleared my head and refocused my attention on only one goal—keep Franco safe. Keep him alive, no matter the risk to myself.

He is all that matters. Not Braulio. Not Jaguar. Not even Diego.

Playing the role of Jaguar's puppet can't help him much in the long run. I need to get to him now. That is the only desire in my skull as I finally pull myself upright and stumble from the bed in the general direction of Jaguar's office. I don't dare turn on the lights in case he can see them from below, so I feel my way through the dark and trip into several heavy objects.

When I finally enter his office, I drop to my hands and knees and scour the area around the desk for anything useful. In his drawers, I find only loose scraps of paper and expensive pens. There is no computer to rummage through, and I don't find his cell phone conveniently in view, either. I could always try his private study, but I doubt I'd be able to make it there unseen.

Suddenly, a louder noise coming from the courtyard draws my attention. It's persistent, uttered in a guttural voice that I instinctively react to even before I creep to the window and spy the source.

Jaguar.

Bathed in the orange glow of outside flood lights, he's standing near the pool, drink in hand, eyes in my direction. "Tiena," he calls. "I know you're awake, chica. Come join us."

Shit.

In his shirt, with my ratty, still damp hair, I feel too vulnerable to expose myself to him and the roughly ten other men and women around him. I will not back down from a direct challenge, either.

So, I improvise. Since the jig is up, I switch on the lights and find my way into the female bedroom next to his suite. In the hallway, I find Horatio, and I wonder if he's been plastered there this whole time, waiting for me. In fact, he could have been the one to alert his master to the fact that I was awake in the first place.

Ignoring him, I enter the bedroom and enter the closet. Luckily for what I have in mind, the space is practically overflowing with string bikinis. Praying that it's at least been washed since its last wearer, I change into a red one, descend the main staircase, and exit the house through the dining room terrace.

He claps when he sees me, seated on a couch-like lounger near the pool. An army of half-naked women encircles him, jostling to get as close to him as they can.

However, at his unspoken command, they all part to make way for me.

"Ah, you look nice and well rested," Jaguar praises, patting the space beside him. "Sleep can do wonders for devious little kitty-vipers. Sit."

I comply, mainly because—despite feeling far better than before—I'm still weak and disoriented. The music playing nearby grates on my throbbing head, and I feel dizzy inhaling so much cheap perfume.

Jaguar, however, seems to feed off the estrogen. "Ladies. Tell Tiena here how much you love hanging out with me."

"We love it here," all six crow in gushing unison.

I'm too tired to put on my unbothered act or remember Pedro's rules for seduction. I wince, cradling my aching temple with one hand. "What am I doing here?" I ask out loud.

Jaguar laughs. "I want your advice on something. Where is that tablet?" He extends his hand, and a simpering blond beside me places the requested device on his lap. "Oh, here it is. Now, which one do you like? We've already voted, and the consensus is this one."

He extends the tablet to me, and I see three snapshots of different mansions. I vaguely remember him viewing something similar earlier. Does he intend to show off his wealth now that he's killed off his last accountant?

I have no desire to help him.

"I'm sure you don't need me to help you make a decision," I say.

An annoyed grunt displaces his charming laugh. "Play along," he says, lowering his voice just for me to hear. "Don't be so spicy, just yet. You are to trust me, remember? As you can see, I take very good care of my toys. Pick."

Biting back a sigh, I inspect the tablet again. The property he'd pointed to as the current frontrunner is an opulent, sprawling villa much like this one. It seems too beautiful to possibly be real. The perfect vehicle to show off a disgusting amount of wealth by a man who makes his fortune off the desperation and exploitation of others.

Spite might be the sole reason I point to its polar opposite among the list of three. On the other hand, I think it may genuinely be my preference—a sleek, modern-style home with large glass windows. Unlike the other option, it gives the allure of stingy modesty. Mystery. When I point to it, I'm satisfied with my choice until a cold, cruel voice in my head whispers—*That's not why you like it. You know why. It's the house he would pick were he given the option.*

Diego.

I shudder, too disgusted to catch all of what Jaguar says next. "…moody for my tastes, but what the lady wants, she gets. The rest of you, clear off, and send out some food for our Tiena. I'm sure she's starving."

He places his hand on my upper thigh, his smile lethal.

"I hope you have an appetite."

"What game is this now, Jaguar?" I ask. God, I could kick myself for not playing along. I know firsthand the danger that comes with pissing him off. For whatever reason, the events of last night have stripped me of my prior armor, and I have nothing left to hide behind.

Diego isn't the sole reason, either. I've fought not to remember what happened between me and the stranger beside me in his private study. He fucked me senseless and then used his mouth on me in ways that would make even

Pedro blush. Then he told me that I had gotten my wish. He wanted me, after all.

If he meant it as a joke, it wouldn't be the first time he humiliated me. He's sadistic as hell, but he's also got a strange sense of humor.

"No game." He pats my thigh gently and leans against the cushions at our back. "No, no… Game would imply that there is something left to be won, but I've already gotten the main prize, haven't I? You. One new woman to add to my harem of six. At least the six I have this week. Tell me, Tiena, will you even last that long?"

He's mocking me, and I can't blame him. At his dismissal, most of his harem has migrated to the pool. They frolic about, aware of all eyes watching them. Beautiful, charming, undeniably perfect women.

"I'm not jealous," I say, still watching them. "And I won't demean these women by claiming to be above them. I'm sure they are all intelligent, and witty, and some may even be more educated than I could ever hope to be. None of them can offer you what I can."

"Oh?" He strokes his chin, his eyes agleam. "And what is that?"

"They don't want you," I say, beating him to the punch. "Not really. Oh, yes, they covet your money, your power, and the ability to stay in your beautiful mansions free of charge. I'm sure they even like to be seen on your periphery, able to bask in a fraction of your influence. None of them really want *you*, Julian Domingas. They wouldn't be so eager to flee from you if they did."

Case and point, none of them look back at our corner, so eager to obey him by ignoring us.

"They fear you," I tell him, confident of the fact. "Maybe not even physically, but emotionally. They know you would gleefully eat their souls for dinner and then move on to the next. They won't ever take that risk."

I don't look over to see how he interprets that statement. Maybe I'm afraid of him, too. Every instinct in my body certainly wants me to be.

With a sigh, he removes his hand from my leg. "Wicked sharp tongue," he scolds. "No wonder Braulio had to beat your ass into submission. I saw the scars."

As another secret comes to light, I wrap my arms around myself to soften the unease. But he's right—if one swaps Braulio for Diego. He beat me mercilessly, and it's only now, a decade on the other side of that hellish relationship, that I can clearly reconcile the violence for what it was. Loathing, not love.

"He did," I confess. "But you haven't. I'm sure there has been a time or two that you have. And I'm sure you've hit other women before. Maybe worse than a slap or two."

Hands like his don't get so calloused for nothing. He reeks of danger, and I am sure he is very capable of displaying it. Unlike Diego, though, I don't think a wild temper is the true motivator behind his flashes of violence.

"You would hit a woman if you knew the fear would benefit you in the long run. Get her to jump the way you wanted. Get her to fear you enough to obey without complaint. You can be very restrained when you want to be, which means you utilize violence only as a weapon. If you thought slapping the shit out of me would truly get me to shut up, you would have. You'd rationalize it as for the greater good, I'm sure."

A low rasp escapes him—a growl masquerading as a laugh. "I could always hit you if I fucking wanted to, Lupe." He reaches out and presses his hand against my face—not hard enough to slap, but gently enough to serve as a warning. "Don't doubt that for a second."

I'm playing with fire in this instance, but I can't help myself.

"You won't," I say. "Because the second you did, there would be nothing separating you from him. A known monster is preferable to the unknown. You would instantly relegate yourself to second best. He would always be first to me. Always."

And maybe I don't know his limits like I want to believe I do. I could be so desperate to escape Diego's memory that I'd try to find the positives in another psychopath for as long as possible. The truth would always reveal itself eventually—they are one and the same.

"You talk a good game," Jaguar says, patting my cheek. Every soft pat becomes a fraction harder, but never a true strike. "I'd warn you to watch that pretty fucking mouth, however, Lupe. We can blame the delirium from the beating you've already taken without me having to lay a single hand on you."

He stands and saunters over to the pool, his arms extended playfully. "Who wants to play a round of chicken?"

His bimbos exclaim gleefully and begin to fight over who can sit on his shoulders first.

Rather than stay and watch, I use what little strength I have left to head inside via the dining room terrace. There, lurking nearby, I find Horatio. His dark eyes rake over me coldly and settle on my lower back.

My wounds throb so badly I'd be concerned if I were in my right mind. For now, I'm just eager to find a place to hide. I start in the direction of the lower level.

"Upstairs," Horatio says before I've even taken a step. "His suite."

Apparently, Jaguar isn't so eager to let me have full reign of his house after all. Still, in this instance, I don't push him. In fact, I think I may have pushed him more than enough. Too far, even.

Damn it. With every passing second, I think some more of my commonsense returns. What am I doing? Needling a bastard I know for a fact has my nephew in his grasp? What if he decided to put Franco in his pet jaguar's cage next? God, I would never forgive myself if it got that far.

You need to get out of this fast, Pita, my intuition warns. Yes. I need to leave. Convince him that I'm not what he wants after all.

Though, I think he's already made that more than clear. I'm not his type, not really. My only interest to Julian Domingas lies in the fact that he thinks another man wants me more.

Desperate to regain my focus, I enter the bathroom and eye my reflection skeptically. *Dios mío.* My forehead has a nasty scratch, and my eyes look sunken. I contort myself enough to spy my back and have to choke down a wave of bile.

It looks so damn bad. How the hell am I walking? Moving?

Maybe because life with Diego taught me to endure pain to an inhuman degree. More than a decade later, my body still remembers how. That thought saddens me. I'm dejected when I reenter Jaguar's office. I don't even have the heart to go through his desk. I just sit in the leather chair behind it and place my face in my hands.

How to get out of this mess?

"It's done."

I look over at the doorway to see Jaguar watching me. For how long? Long enough that he's lost the playful smirk he wore around his bimbos. My misery is boring him.

"My gift for you," he clarifies. "Once you go to sleep again, you will wake up as if this has been one bad, bad dream, Lupe. I've made your wish come true for the time being—I promise you that. I will need to drug you, though. I hope you don't take offense."

"Drug me. For what?" That request has so many horrific implications that I can't even fathom them all at once. Stunned, I blurt, "So I can wake up in Gatita's cage again?"

"No," he says coldly. "So that I can uphold our bargain, Lupe. You want my protection? Your son safe from harm? Then you'll understand that discretion is vital, and you'll take the pill I offer you like the good girl I know you can be."

Discretion? He does intend to move me somewhere, it seems. Horrified by the prospect, my reply is hoarse, "How can I trust you?"

His eyes flash to remind me of the promise I myself made to him. *You will have all of me.*

"Luckily for you, Tiena, trust isn't what I want from you this time. Take the drug or not. It's your choice. I do have another request, however. This one is nonnegotiable. Think of it as payment for the good deeds I've done for you."

He advances, his hands at his sides, head cocked at a dangerous angle. "Will you refuse?"

"What is it?" I croak, breathless.

He reaches the desk and leans over it, bracing his hands before him. "I need to better understand your dynamic with *Braulio*," he says, stressing that name in a way that makes me shiver. "So, I want you to fuck me again—but none of that selfish, detached nonsense you're so good at. I want you to fuck me the way you fucked him. Back when you loved him oh so much. Can you do that?"

My stomach lurches. Sex isn't what scares me about this proposition. Fuck him like I fucked Diego? Oh, God, no. Never. That is one secret regarding Julian Domingas that I will take to the grave. It was always better sexually with him. He doesn't seem to realize that.

Can I even put on a show that could convince him otherwise?

"When?" I ask, hoping to buy more time.

No such luck.

"Now," he says coldly. "This isn't a standing invitation."

I purse my lips to hide my disappointment. "You see the state I'm in."

"Ah, yes. The state of you…" He runs his thumb from my jawline to my forehead and frowns at what he sees. "Don't pretend like you even feel the pain, Lupe. You carry yourself like a warrior, numb to it all. In fact, don't ever use pain as an excuse around me." He swats my face away from him, though not violently. "If you've changed your mind, then say so now. I won't waste any more resources on a sly, manipulative little bitch who can't back up her big words with action."

Ouch. He meant the insult that time, and it rightfully stings.

"I will only make the offer one last time—"

"Okay," I say, palming the desk, desperate to disguise how my hands shake. "Eat with me first. I'm starving and can't take a drug on an empty stomach."

His eyes narrow but his smirk returns.

Standing, I follow him into his bedroom, where he activates an intercom system built into the wall and demands food be brought to us.

Not even five minutes later, two scantily-clad women enter the room with trays of assorted appetizers and fruits.

"Take your pick," Jaguar taunts me. "I'm curious what foods a viper-kitty prefers."

I take a small, delicate cucumber sandwich in one hand and a strawberry in the other. I eat them sloppily—ravenously— and he watches on, laughing all the while.

"Don't choke yourself, chica. That's what I intend for you to do on my cock alone."

My cheeks burn in response to that comment, and in true predator style, he pounces.

"Braulio never had you suck him off." Rather than smug, he sounds skeptical.

It's partly true. Diego preferred to put his cock in other orifices on my body. My pussy. My ass when the mood struck him. My mouth was better utilized uttering praises to him until my voice went hoarse.

"Some men like to slake their needs in other ways," I say carefully.

"You're a damn liar. From the second I first met you, I've been wondering how deep down that throat you can take me. I think it may be the only way a man could get you to shut the hell up."

Ah. So he's still bitter about our poolside discussion. In this instance, I don't rush to soothe his ego. I keep eating.

I keep stalling.

Think. Think. Fuck him like he thinks I fucked my fictional version of Braulio. He's after something specific. A set of reactions vastly different from how I've been with him. But how?

Damn it. My minuscule arsenal of sexual escapades isn't anywhere grand enough to please him.

"You seem worried, Lupe," Jaguar scolds. "Afraid that Braulio will get wind of you exposing your secret playbook? Believe me, sweetheart, there is nothing that I haven't seen."

He doesn't seem to think he's wrong, but I suspect I can name what he doesn't understand and wouldn't recognize. True affection. Love, not lust.

If only I knew what that was. My knowledge in that arena is as limited as his seems to be. What would Pedro suggest I do in this instance? It's simple. Improvise.

So, I call upon a knowledge that I once was ashamed of— the handful of romance novels I used to read during my time with Diego to keep myself sane. I would compare our "love" to the relationships between those fictional characters, and I would lie to myself that it was the same thing. They were passionate. Respectful. Understanding of each other's limitations.

Oh God, young Pita was such a damn fool. But those sad little fantasies may be all that can help me now.

"You've eaten enough," Jaguar says, once I've swallowed my fourth cucumber sandwich. "As you like to point out, I am a busy man. I have other matters to attend to. Besides, this shouldn't take long. I'm sure Braulio lasted what? Ten minutes on a good day?"

I let the barb slip past unchallenged. Slowly I rise to my feet and approach the bed. With hungry footsteps, he follows.

"You let me set the pace," I say, to preface this demonstration. "I control it—"

"Enough talking Lupe," he warns. "I want action."

So, I step into him and press my mouth to his.

Our last kiss was a brief, thrilling display of his chaotic preference when it comes to intimacy. He likes it rough. Hard. Fast. No strings attached, and kissing isn't high on his list.

But if I were to devise my ultimate lover, he would make me enjoy this act. He would go slow and savor me. He would stroke my tongue and palm my waist in his hands so that I felt safe. Protected. Needed.

Jaguar grunts in amusement as I attempt to forge such a scenario with him. It should be awkward to implement. Pathetic beyond belief.

Instead, it feels…

Almost real. If I close my eyes and pretend, another man could be in his place, carefully following my lead.

I let my mind run rampant and devise new aspects of this imaginary man.

He's roughly the same size as Jaguar, with muscles that he would love for me to stroke and explore at my leisure. They'd feel like living stone beneath my fingertips, so hard it seems impossible for them to be capable of any kindness.

But he would *only* utilize kindness with me.

He'd like me to take the lead and push him back until he has no choice but to sit on the bed. Then he'd let me mount him.

A laugh trickles from Jaguar's throat, to undercut the make-believe. To my utter shock, he complies anyway, lying back so I can straddle him. I push the real man from my head and replace him with his fictional counterpart.

Let's call him… Bob.

Bob would love for me to undress him, hunched over his waist reverently. He'd be as beautiful as a certain narco is, large enough to fill the width of my hand. Pulsing and warm, and I'd relish the feel of him. Holding him. Pressing my lips to his tip.

He'd like that, and would issue a growl of approval in the base of his throat—the fact that I hear a very real one is merely my overactive imagination.

Yes.

Back to the fantasy…

Or not. Every time I try to erect a mental barrier in my mind, the real Julian Domingas does something to shatter it. Panicked, I switch gears. My dream man just happens to look like him. Sound like him. Feel the way he does.

I wouldn't take him in my mouth, this perfect man. He wouldn't want that. This moment would be for me alone. He'd understand my prior abuse and would endeavor to make sure I felt only safe with him. Needed. He would gladly relinquish the reins to me.

Naturally, that means he wouldn't throw me down and climb on top of me like a brute. He would let me ride him instead.

I would do so boldly, armed with the confidence that comes from being truly loved. He would love me—this man would. God, how he would love me.

He'd hiss out praises as I slid onto his cock and rocked to take him deeper. He'd suck in a breath as my eyes rolled, and I threw my head back to adjust to the feel of him.

My perfect lover would let me take all the time I needed. He wouldn't rush. He'd even let me grab his hands and explore them via touch for long, leisurely seconds. Christ, he would have such dangerous, rugged hands.

In real time, I run my fingers along the palms and individual knuckles. Then I bring one set of digits to my mouth and suck on one merely to gauge what he tastes like. Violence. Danger.

No—he tastes like perfection. Passion. Lust for me.

He'd do anything for me.

Only when I was ready would I begin to move, rocking my hips slowly. Slowly. Then harder when I needed to feel him…

There.

I'd cry loudly at the pleasure he could give me—a fire unlike any other. I'd chase it mindlessly, knowing he'd follow. I'd press his hand to my chest and let him feel how fast my heart is racing. How good he's making me feel.

I'd say his name…

But that would be too dangerous now. So, I just gasp and gasp, bearing my hips onto his, rocking the entire bed with our movements.

The man beneath me would only be able to restrain himself for so long before his groans of ecstasy joined mine. Low. Guttural. Beautiful fucking noises.

Drunk on pleasure, I'd show him my gratitude for giving me such power. I'd hunch over him and press my lips to his throat. Feather kisses down his chest and smooth my fingers along his perfect, flawless skin.

However, the painted flesh I find beneath my searching fingertips fractures my fantasy. This calls for a rewrite—my perfect man has tattoos. Endless tattoos, made of black ink and delicate swirls. Then skulls. A snarling Jaguar behind a thicket of leaves.

He would have his secrets, but I'd love him more for it. My perfect lover. He would never keep anything from me.

And I would share all of myself with him. All of it. I wouldn't let fear keep me from exploring him. Worshiping him. Taking my pleasure.

Intoxicated by him, I'd press open mouth kisses to his chest and trace the tattoos nearest me.

And he would…

Groan. Buck his hips into me, driving his cock into my inner walls. He couldn't help himself.

And I would allow him that fracturing bit of control. I'd crave him even more for it. His coming undone would only herald an orgasm for the ages. For both of us. We'd feel it coming like a freight train with no way of stopping it.

I'd go first, eyes rolling, toes curling, voice echoing throughout the room like a mad woman's.

And just as loudly, he'd follow, gripping my hips so hard he'd bruise and using the leverage to slam into me. So hard. So fast.

His strength would make the headboard slam into the wall, and we'd hit that peak together. Hot. Breathless. Mindless. Climax.

Utterly spent, I'd collapse against him, pressing my lips to his neck. His chest. I wouldn't be able to get enough of him…

"Enough." The low rasp of Julian Domingas snaps me back to reality.

Hard.

Blinking, I realize that it's *his* body I've been mouthing. *Dios mío.* I scramble off him, crawling to the other side of the bed, my cheeks flaming.

"Wait," he warns before I can even think to stand.

Reaching toward the nightstand, he picks up something he must have prepared for this moment. "Open," he commands, beckoning me with a crooked finger.

He means my mouth. When I comply, he places something on my tongue. Hard. Round.

The promised pill.

I swallow it dryly and tell myself I'm not afraid as it slides down my throat.

"Braulio is more of a fucking pussy than I thought," Jaguar says, leaning back against the pillows, his hands folded behind his head. "He likes it mushy."

And he doesn't. Not that I try to let his amusement sting. My fictional Bob would have my appreciation far more than the two other men I've been with. I think I mourn for him. Poor fake Bob.

"What now?" I ask Jaguar when he doesn't move.

"You?" He inclines his head toward me, an eyebrow raised. "You sleep. Lie down like a good girl. I'll wait here until you drift off."

It doesn't sound like a comforting gesture. Still, left with no choice, I lie down anyway, putting my back to him.

He laughs, but doesn't make a move to touch me.

"I think I'd beat the shit out of you as well," he says in a dangerous voice. "If doing so made you fuck me like that every night. I'm not a fan, but I don't deny…" He chuckles, but his genuine appreciation laces his tone—and fury. Without warning, he must snatch a piece of my hair, tugging hard. "Those noises you made gave you away. You've been faking it with me, after all this time, Tiena. Dirty *fucking liar.*"

I shiver, unnerved. There's no use in arguing with him. So, I don't. "Was I?" I ask.

I wouldn't know.

"Go to sleep, *Tiena*," he says, letting me go. "I'll think up a fitting punishment for you, though. I'll have all the time in the world to learn what makes you scream."

That doesn't sound good.

"I can think of one way," I tell him hoarsely. "Fuck me like your dream woman, and we'll call it even. You held back with me too."

"Ah… But I never promised you my soul, did I? I never promised you shit. Honesty is how you curry favor with me, *Tiena*. Not threats."

He has a point. Dear God, he has a point.

As delirious as I am, that statement triggers a reaction from me I can't suppress. When I eventually wake up, I'll know better than to hope I'll find the sweet dreams he promised me.

I'll only discover a new phase to this nightmare, and Jaguar will be waiting for me, ready to devour me whole.

But this time, I want it to be on my terms, however fragile they may be.

"I'm not Tiena," I croak, my voice muffled, eyes drifting shut despite how fiercely I struggle to stay coherent. Still, I manage to push out two more words, though I have no idea how they land. "…I'm Lupita."

~ Continue Jaguar and Lupita's story in Blood Debt ~

A WORD FROM THE AUTHOR

Hey there!

Thank you so much for reading! If you enjoyed the story, please leave a review and recommend the book to any friend you think would love this twisted world. You'd have my eternal gratitude. Even a short sentence goes a long way!

Then, come join the rest of us dark romance lovers in my Facebook Group where you can get snippets, sneak peeks of upcoming books and even help vote on aspects of future novels.

Come to the dark side:
https://www.facebook.com/groups/lanasbeautifulmonsters/

WANT MORE STUFF TO READ?
Join my newsletter and get a **free book**! Plus, you get to stay updated with any new releases, random giveaways and exclusive sneak peeks!
https://www.lanaskybooks.com/newsletter

Other Novels: https://lanaskybooks.com/

ABOUT THE AUTHOR

Lana Sky is a reclusive writer in the United States who spends most of her time daydreaming about complex male characters and parenting her Cockapoo Joey. She writes dark, twisted romance across several genres. Her titles include everything from mafia romance to vampires.

facebook.com/AuthorLanaSky

twitter.com/lanasky101

amazon.com/author/lanasky

pinterest.com/lanasky101

goodreads.com/lanasky

instagram.com/lanasky101

bookbub.com/authors/lana-sky

tiktok.com/@author_lana_sky